"I'm glad we've had this chance to speak to each other."

"So am I. Perhaps sometime we will have another opportunity, and you can tell me more about your family."

He nodded. "I would like that."

A rattling of pans came faintly from the kitchen, and they both looked down the hall, then back at each other.

Étienne held out his hand. Letitia hesitated, then leaned over the railing and clasped it. She tried not to recall her father's adamant words: *I thought you understood my feelings about LeClair.*

"I must go," he all but whispered. "Perhaps I shall see you at church tomorrow."

"Yes."

They stood gazing at each other for another long moment, and her pulse cavorted wildly. Then he gave a nod, as though he completely understood her chaotic feelings, and turned to leave.

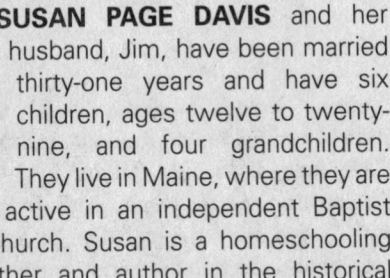

SUSAN PAGE DAVIS and her husband, Jim, have been married thirty-one years and have six children, ages twelve to twenty-nine, and four grandchildren. They live in Maine, where they are active in an independent Baptist church. Susan is a homeschooling mother and author in the historical romance, fantasy, and romantic suspense genres. Visit her Web site at www.susanpagedavis.com.

Books by Susan Page Davis

Don't miss out on any of our super romances. Write to us at the following address for information on our newest releases and club information.

Heartsong Presents Readers' Service
PO Box 721
Uhrichsville, OH 44683

Or visit www.heartsongpresents.com

The Lumberjack's Lady

Susan Page Davis

Heartsong Presents

To my sister, Pat, *qui a le courage lire mes romans*. You helped me learn to read and taught me my first few words of French. You didn't proof this page, so if I phrased something wrong, it's my fault. I can forgive the many times you scared the wits out of me (we're talking apple-burger stand here, as well as dire predictions about Duke and Duchess eating children alive). And in case you're still wondering, the estate papers prove I am NOT adopted. As we used to say, "Sailor leave-ra." Sisters forever!

A note from the Author:
I love to hear from my readers! You may correspond with me by writing:

Susan P. Davis
Author Relations
PO Box 721
Uhrichsville, OH 44683

ISBN 978-1-59789-587-3

THE LUMBERJACK'S LADY

All scripture quotations are taken from the King James Version of the Bible.

All of the characters and events in this book are fictitious. Any resemblance to actual persons, living or dead, or to actual events is purely coincidental.

Our mission is to publish and distribute inspirational products offering exceptional value and biblical encouragement to the masses.

PRINTED IN THE U.S.A.

one

Maine, 1895

Étienne LeClair bounded down the steps of the lumber camp's bunkhouse and headed for the stable. Marise, the cook, needed supplies, but the lumberjack didn't look forward to driving to the nearest town, twelve miles away. The January sun held no warmth, and the bitter-cold morning air chilled his lungs. He would rather be at his usual duty of felling trees with the other men.

However, the big boss was here, come all the way up from his fine home in the city a hundred or more miles away to inspect the operation. Perhaps it was better not to be working in the cut when Lincoln Hunter was on hand.

As he crossed the yard to the stable where the sturdy draft horses were housed, a sharp scream reached his ears.

Étienne stopped and turned toward the distant sound. In a fraction of a second, his brain registered the woman's voice. It was not the tone of the rotund camp cook, Marise. But there were no other women in the lumber camp. Or there hadn't been until yesterday.

He caught his breath. The boss's daughter!

He sprinted toward the woods behind the bunkhouse, searching for a hint of her whereabouts. Beneath the trees he stopped and listened. Over the sighing of the bare branches above, a thrashing noise reached him. He ran on, straight toward it.

"Mademoiselle?" he called as he broke through the trees to a frozen little pond in the woods.

"Here! Help me, please!"

He saw her then, at the far side of the pond, standing a little more than waist deep in a hole in the ice, the broken chunks sliding around her as she tried to climb out. Her futile movements were clumsy as she tried to raise a knee to the edge of the surface.

"Wait, mademoiselle!" he shouted, and she turned toward his voice.

Panic was etched on her face. Even from a distance he had an impression of vivid blue eyes like her father's. Wisps of light brown hair fluttered about her face. She tried once more to climb up out of the hole, but the edge of the ice broke beneath her weight, plunging her, prone, into the frigid water.

"Mademoiselle Hunter!"

He charged around the edge of the pond, not daring to trust the ice to hold him up. She surfaced and batted the edge of the ice sheet with her hands, encased in sodden wool gloves, floundering as she tried to stand. Her frightened eyes searched him out and stared toward him in mute appeal as she choked and sputtered.

When he was as close to her as he could get on solid footing, he grabbed a sapling for support and leaned out toward her.

"Mademoiselle, can you reach my hand?"

She stretched toward him, her hand extending toward his but not quite meeting it. If she didn't grasp his fingers within seconds, he knew he would have to plunge in and get her, but that would endanger them both. It might be too hard for him to climb out again carrying her, and the frigid water would sap his strength in seconds.

"Come to me, *mon amie*," he said softly.

Her pupils flared, and she took one lunge of a step and launched herself in his direction. As her body met the broken edge of the ice and once more her weight caused it to give beneath her, he grabbed for her wrist and caught it as her head went under.

He pulled her upward, holding the springy young tree with his other hand and praying it would not crack under the stress. Miss Hunter surfaced and stared at him, terror in her eyes.

With painful slowness he drew her in, but her soaked clothing dragged her down, and it took all his strength to pull her to the bank. At last she stood just below him, clinging to his arm. He stooped and lifted her, setting her down on a fallen log near the bank.

Her teeth chattered violently, and water streamed from her skirt and coat. She had no hat, or if she'd worn one, it was gone now. Her bedraggled scarf hung limp and dripping, sagging toward the frozen ground, but he knew it would freeze stiff within minutes. Quickly he unwound it so that it would not put any pressure on her neck. Then he noticed the steel skate blades clamped to her shoes.

"Here, mademoiselle." He stripped off his warm wool jacket and wrapped it around her shoulders. Even in her own wet coat, she could fit inside it, and he yanked his gloves off so he could fasten the top button, then snatched his hat off his head, pulled down the ear flaps, and settled it over her matted hair.

"Can you walk?" he asked.

She stared up at him, her eyes not quite focusing on him. That vacant gaze frightened him, and he tossed aside the reservations that normally would have kept him from touching the boss's daughter.

He bent and enfolded her in his arms.

"Place your arms around my neck."

She blinked at him. He thought she would not respond any further, but slowly she raised her hands. Her gloves were rapidly freezing, and drops hanging from the fingertips congealed into little icicles. He grabbed her gloves, peeled them from her stiff hands, and threw them to the ground, stooping for his own discarded gloves. They were drier than hers, though not much. He slid them over her hands, and she raised them to his collarbone then over his shoulders. The cold wind sliced through his flannel shirt and union suit, and when the frozen gloves touched the skin at the back of his neck, he flinched.

"Hold on now. I will take you back." His face was very close to hers, and he noticed the drops of water frozen on her dark lashes. When she blinked, the ice droplets touched her cheek, and she frowned.

He delayed no longer but lifted her bodily and strode for the bunkhouse, one long step after another. She was heavier than he'd expected. Strands of her hair escaped from beneath his cap and mingled with his beard, freezing together against his chin. He shook his head to dislodge them, but when he did it she moaned and sank lower in his arms. He gritted his teeth and hurried on, not pausing until he reached the step at the back door of the kitchen.

He couldn't knock, and he wouldn't set her down, so he raised one foot and kicked a tattoo against the lower boards of the door. After waiting a few seconds, he thumped again with his boot, and at last the door flew open.

"What is it? Étienne! That's the young lady. Oh, my sakes, what happened to her?" Marise, the foreman's wife who cooked for the lumbering crew all winter, clapped a hand to her cheek.

"She fell through the ice." Étienne grunted.

Marise sidestepped, holding the door wide. "Bring her in! Hurry."

Étienne's strength was ebbing, but he managed to lug Miss Hunter to the small room behind the kitchen that was allotted to her for the duration of her visit. It was the only private chamber away from the men's quarters overhead. Usually Marise and her husband, Robert, occupied it, but they had given it up for the young lady's convenience and were sleeping on bunks curtained off from the rest of the open barracks above, as was Mr. Hunter.

Miss Hunter's eyes were closed now. Marise tugged off the cap and gloves that Étienne had forced on her and then began to ease her out of his wool jacket.

"Oh, the clothes! Her coat is soaked. Help me."

Étienne lifted the young lady once more and helped Marise tug the saturated sleeves from her arms.

"We must get her warm," the cook muttered. She glanced at Étienne. "Yes, and you need to get warm, too. Your hands are stiff, no?"

He nodded.

"Build up the kitchen fire," Marise said. "Warm yourself and heat the kitchen. Once I get her into dry things, we will take her out there."

There was no fireplace in the small chamber, and Étienne knew Marise's plan made sense. He staggered to the kitchen, fed some sticks into the low blaze in the cookstove, and held his hands over the open cover of the firebox, flexing his fingers. When they had stopped stinging and he could function better, he built up a fire from the coals in the big fireplace of the dining hall, too, and stoked the blaze there.

The kitchen grew warmer, and his shivering subsided. His hands still ached, but he shook off the mild pain. What would Mademoiselle Hunter feel when she awoke? Her pain would be far more intense. He sent up a silent prayer for her and walked down the short hall to the door of the chamber where she lay.

Marise was shaking out a wool blanket and spreading it over the form on the bunk. "It's warm out there?"

"Yes."

The cook nodded. "You carry her then. I will drag the tick out there for her."

Étienne approached the bunk and looked down at the young woman's face, now in repose. *So beautiful,* he thought. *And so vulnerable.*

"Is she unconscious?" he whispered.

"Sleeping. She was all worn out, poor thing!" Marise had stripped the young woman's wet clothing from her and some-how gotten a dry flannel gown onto her. Although the ice had melted from her lashes and hair, the air was still chilly, and her face was marble white. He stooped to gather her in his arms, and she let out a soft moan. He lifted her, straightening his knees. Marise tucked the edges of the striped blanket around the girl, and he gathered them in.

She was much lighter than before. The sodden coat and other clothing must have accounted for much of the staggering burden that had hindered him earlier. No wonder it had been impossible for her to drag herself out of the hole in the pond, carrying that load and battling numbness in her limbs.

He carried her to the kitchen, and Marise came behind, pulling the straw-filled mattress from the bunk and placing it close to the stove, not close enough to scorch her skin but near enough for her to feel the radiating warmth.

He knelt and deposited Miss Hunter gently on top of the white linen sheet Marise had smoothed over the straw tick. She settled with a soft sigh.

"She needs her pillow," Marise said.

Étienne rose and headed back to the small chamber.

"And bring another blanket," the cook called after him.

It took him a minute to locate the cupboard where extra bedding was stored. He chose a creamy Hudson Bay blanket with red stripes along one edge because it stood out from the other plain, dark ones.

Foolishness, he thought. *What does the color of a blanket matter?*

When he returned, Marise was bustling about the cookstove. "I am making tea for her, and broth."

He nodded and knelt beside the sleeping woman again. Her damp hair was matted to her temples, but tendrils were drying and separating. He slipped his hand beneath her head and lifted it, sliding the feather pillow underneath. He and the other men slept without pillows and were thankful to have lumpy straw ticks. But this was a delicate young lady, and he supposed she needed a softer place to rest her head.

He couldn't resist brushing back a wisp of hair, dark with

dampness, but lightening as it dried. She didn't look like the boss, whose shrewdness showed in his sharp nose and jutting jaw. Étienne knew she had the same intense blue eyes as her father; he'd had opportunity to stare into their depths as he pulled her from the pond. But her cold, pale face held a rounded sweetness that was more than youth. She was beautiful.

Étienne had not seen her before the encounter at the pond. Last night when the men returned from the woods after spending all day working at the cut, they had learned that the boss and his lovely daughter had arrived and would be in camp for a couple of days. Mr. Hunter had spoken to the men after supper, but the young lady was nowhere to be seen.

Now he wondered how the boss dared to bring her to his lumber camps. Hunter came around every year to take a firsthand look at operations, but he'd always brought a male clerk. Never a woman, and especially not a young, beautiful woman. The forty rough men who lived in this camp for the winter didn't see women for months at a time, other than dumpy Marise, who was nearly as tough and outspoken as her husband. Marise wouldn't take any nonsense from the crew. But a pretty young lady like this?

She stirred, and Étienne drew back, still gazing at her. Under ordinary circumstances, he would scarcely dare to look at her, and then only covertly, from a distance. He was a humble workman, and a French Canadian at that. He would never speak to such a lady, let alone touch her. Yet today, he had done both, and here she was lying helpless.

He turned to Marise, a sudden panic in his chest. "She will be all right, won't she?"

"Oh, yes, she is not a weakling, this one. But she has been shocked, you know. She needs rest. And she may take cold."

"I tried to keep her warm."

"You did well. Don't fret so."

He swallowed hard and looked down at the mademoiselle's

face again. Was he imagining it or was the color returning to her cheeks? Her lashes were dry now, lying soft and feathery against the light skin.

Marise came toward him carrying a steaming cup with a spoon handle protruding from it. "Her father will thank you; be sure of that."

Étienne stood up, suddenly in turmoil. "Her father! We must tell him."

"I sent Jean Charles."

He exhaled in relief. The blacksmith. Marise must have summoned Jean Charles while he was getting the bedding. He was glad he didn't have to go in search of Mr. Hunter. He didn't want to see the anger and fear in the man's eyes when he learned his daughter had been in mortal danger. And he wanted to stay beside the mademoiselle as long as he was permitted. But still, if the boss was already being told of the mishap, he would be here soon.

Dread and misgiving fluttered in his chest, and he inhaled deeply. No one liked to be singled out by the boss. Mr. Hunter was a hard man whose one passion in life was his business. It was true he admired and praised men who worked hard, but he couldn't tolerate those who were lazy or clumsy or wasteful. Was he tender toward his only daughter? He might be upset that she had come into such peril, and if so, he might look for someone to blame. Étienne did not want the man's scrutiny directed at him.

"I had better get on with my errand."

Marise went to her knees beside the young woman and set the cup down beside her. "Yes, go. I need those supplies before supper. Especially the sugar."

Étienne knew how unhappy the other men would be if they did not get the sweets Marise produced for dessert each evening. The rich foods gave them the energy they needed to perform their grueling work and ward off the cold.

"Here now." Marise stroked the young woman's cheek. "Miss

Hunter, can you hear me? You need to take some tea. That's it. *Bien!*"

The young woman's lashes fluttered and rose, and Étienne caught his breath. Yes, her eyes were as blue as the eggs of the red-winged blackbird.

She looked at Marise, then shifted her gaze upward and found him.

He smiled. "Mademoiselle is feeling better?"

"You. . ." It was only a whisper, and her forehead furrowed.

"Here, now. Take this." Marise held a spoonful of liquid to the young woman's lips.

Étienne turned and slipped out the door, sending a prayer of praise heavenward.

two

Letitia Hunter woke in a small room with rough board walls. Raising her head off the pillow, she recognized the little chamber in the bunkhouse at Spruce Run Camp, where she'd slept last night. She sat up. Hadn't she been in the kitchen? She recalled the plump cook bending over her. Her hands and feet ached. With a sudden lurch of terror, she remembered the pond.

Her gaze fell on the bedside table, and there were her steel skate runners. She had clamped them to her shoes with such joyful anticipation! The chance to glide across the ice of the little wooded pond had beckoned her, and for a few glorious seconds, she had felt like a child again.

A soft knock sounded on the door, and she pulled the woolen blanket around her. "Come in."

Marise entered, carrying a steaming mug and a small plate.

"Bien! I hoped mademoiselle was awake. You feel better now?"

As the cook set the dishes down, Letitia saw that the cup held a dark liquid and the plate a pair of dainty pastries.

Marise smiled at her. "I put lots of sugar in the tea."

"Thank you." Letitia hadn't the heart to tell her she drank her tea plain. "I was foolish, wasn't I? I nearly got myself killed, and I suspect you've been tending me."

"It is nothing. But your father, he is worried."

"He carried me in here, didn't he?"

"Yes, after we knew you were warmed up and would be all right here in this cool room. And he sat by your bedside for an hour."

"Really?" Letitia had some difficulty imagining such tenderness in her father. When she was little, yes, but Mother was alive then. Lately he'd been distant and businesslike.

"He is out in the dining hall now, waiting to see the man who rescued you."

Letitia frowned. "I. . .remember. He was a big man."

Marise smiled and bobbed her head. "Étienne LeClair. He is a fine man and strong as a young ox. He pulled you from the water and brought you here."

"I must thank him."

"I'm certain you will have the opportunity. Now you take a bit of refreshment and rest some more."

Letitia picked up the tea and took a small sip. As she had feared, it was far too sweet. She set the cup down. In her mind, she saw the muscular lumberjack clinging to a sapling and leaning out over the water toward her. "Come to me," he'd said, and she'd wanted to, more than anything. She'd looked up into his rich brown eyes, and for a split second she'd forgotten about her peril. She'd noticed only those wide, steady eyes.

"He had beautiful eyes." She saw the cook's surprise and laughed. "I'm sorry. It's just that when I was in the freezing water and I thought I'd never get out, he came to help me—and I thought his eyes were the most beautiful things I'd ever seen."

Marise nodded solemnly.

She thinks I'm very silly, Letitia thought. *But when I see Étienne LeClair again, I shall let him know how grateful I am. I shall never forget his kindness or his eyes.*

"Mademoiselle should rest now."

Marise padded from the room and closed the door, but Letitia knew she couldn't sleep anymore. She rose and reached for the stool beside the bed as her knees wobbled, threatening to betray her. She pulled in a careful breath and eyed her clothes hanging from pegs on the opposite wall. If she were cautious, she felt sure she could get them and dress herself.

&

The sun hung low behind the dark fir trees when Étienne returned to the Spruce Run Camp. The horses were tired from the long trip, and the biting cold air had frozen the sweat on the shaggy winter hair of their flanks. Étienne led them into the stable, and Jean Charles came to help him unharness the team.

"You had better get that sugar to the kitchen, *vite!*"

Étienne raised his eyebrows. "Marise, she is fretting?"

"Ah, you've no idea. She is making a special dish for the boss, and she is blackening your name for being so long with her sugar. Go. I will do this."

Étienne smiled. Marise's frequent tirades were meaningless. He hefted two twenty-pound sacks of sugar from the wagon bed.

"*Merci.* I will be back to unload the rest."

When he entered through the back door, he was relieved to see that Mademoiselle Hunter had been moved out of the kitchen but disappointed that he did not have another glimpse of her.

"Ah! The sugar." Marise pounced on the first sack as soon as he thumped it onto her worktable, cutting the coarse thread that bound the top closed. Étienne set the other sack down in a corner.

"The mademoiselle, she is better?"

"Yes, she is resting. But you need to go in there." Marise nodded toward the dining hall.

"I have more to unload."

"Later. The boss, he wants to see you."

A salvo of apprehension slammed Étienne in the chest. He stooped and looked through the gap above the counter where she served them their meals into the large dining room beyond. Huddled in a chair at the table nearest the stone fireplace sat gray-haired Mr. Hunter, cradling a stoneware mug in his hands.

"Go." Marise plunged a tin measuring cup into the sugar. "He has been waiting a long time. First he sat by his daughter's side, but after we moved her into the back room again and she went to sleep, he came out and stayed in the dining hall. I took him biscuits and coffee, but that is not what he needs. Go."

Étienne took off his gloves and shoved them into his pockets, then reached up and pulled off his cap. Would the boss be angry? He brushed a hand over his hair to smooth it down. Probably he just wanted to hear Étienne's account of what had happened.

Maybe he wonders why I was nearby to help her, he thought. *Maybe he thinks I was watching her, thinking to harm her.*

He gulped air that seemed suddenly thick and unwieldy. One tried not to be noticed by the boss. Not that he was harsh, but when he came out to the cut, the men were on edge as his bright, piercing eyes took in every swing of the ax, every adjustment on the harnesses and chains as the teamsters prepared for their horses to twitch the logs out, dragging them over the ground. Sometimes Hunter gave praise, and that was a good thing. But sometimes his face darkened, and he would speak to the foreman. Then Robert would curse at them and order them about with an arrogance that said, "It's not my fault, Mr. Hunter, that the men, they are so stupid. It's not my fault they are doing it wrong. It's not my fault they are slow and clumsy."

None of this was spoken, but it made the lumberjacks and teamsters feel less than men. And it made them resent Robert. It also made them wonder if Mr. Hunter had ever held an ax in his hands. He was good at running a sawmill and selling lumber, yes, but could he fell a tree on a dime or limb logs all day? Probably the boss's hands would blister in five minutes if he tried to do what they did.

The men had good times in camp, but the boss's visits were not those times. After Mr. Hunter had left, that would be the time when they relaxed in the evenings and brought out their checkerboards. Michael would play his fiddle. They would laugh and tell stories and eat Marise's doughnuts and feel happy to be here. But not while the boss remained in camp.

"Would you go?"

Marise's sharp hiss prodded him. Étienne squared his shoulders and pushed through the swinging door to the dining hall.

❧

Letitia struggled with her buttons. Her fingers still ached, but she forced them to function, determined to dress and take dinner with her father. The best way to banish his concern was to prove she had recovered from her mishap.

She probed the back of her hair and found only a few hairpins left in her tresses. No doubt the rest were at the bottom of that wretched pond. One would think, with the cold weather, that the pond would have been solid ice from surface to leafy bottom. But according to Marise, it hadn't been so awfully cold until the last two days. She supposed that the evergreens had sheltered the pond from the wind and kept it from freezing clear through. She reached for her hairbrush.

Father would probably forbid her from skating again. He would certainly regret bringing her with him on his annual trip into the northern Maine woods.

He'd caught her off guard the day after Christmas when he announced that she would accompany him. She was shocked that he would take her into the seven lumber camps the Northern Lumber Company maintained.

Usually when he traveled to his far-flung camps, he took his chief clerk with him to keep records and take care of correspondence. But this year the elderly clerk, Oscar Weston, was retiring, and he had told her father with more force than he normally employed that he would not traipse about the lumber camps again this winter. His rheumatism had taken enough of that, thank you. Her father had managed to persuade Weston to postpone his retirement and run the office while he was away, and then he had told Letitia to pack her bag, as she was coming along to clerk for him.

At first she had balked at leaving the comparative comfort of home in the dead of winter, but she knew there was no getting around it. When her father made up his mind, that was that.

Of course, there had been two clerks in the Northern Lumber Company office. But the second clerk had been dismissed when her father discovered that the figures in his ledger did not agree with those in the orders received.

Rather than hire another man, Lincoln Hunter had pressed his daughter into service. She was quick with figures, patient, and able to make a decent cup of coffee to offer clients. He had assured her that the position would be temporary, but nearly two years had passed—and as far as Letitia could see, her father had made no effort to find another clerk. She had worked in the office with old Mr. Weston, learning every aspect of the business's paperwork: orders, accounts, correspondence, price lists, and shipping schedules. A sigh escaped her, and she wondered if she would ever get away from the office.

Then a smile touched her lips. This trip was a good thing, she decided, as she pulled the brush through her long hair. It gave her a chance, on the train ride and the long wagon trips between camps, to talk to her father. At home, he never sat still long enough for that. She hoped he was beginning to understand that she wanted a home and family of her own one day. She did not want to finish her life as a retired spinster clerk.

Since her mother's death, Letitia's social circle had shrunk. For the most part, her father had stopped inviting people to their home. If he wanted to entertain a client, he bought him dinner at one of the town's best hotels. When she began working full time in the office, Letitia's isolation had increased. She saw only the clients, Mr. Weston, and the other employees of Northern Lumber.

Her closest friend was now Angelique Laplante, wife of the lumberyard foreman. Letitia often visited in the Laplantes' modest home on Sundays. She sensed that her father wouldn't approve if he knew, but she found the boisterous family buoyed her spirits and encouraged her in her spiritual walk.

The last button in place, she smoothed the soft skirt of her blue wool dress. There was no mirror in the chamber. Apparently Marise never needed to check her appearance. Letitia took her hand mirror from her valise and surveyed her reflection. Her face was still pale, but otherwise she looked fine.

A sudden flash of memory hit her, and once more she saw the kind brown eyes of the lumberjack looking down at her in the kitchen. She rummaged in the valise. Where was the blue ribbon that matched this dress?

She stopped and scolded herself. Vanity. Most likely she and Father would leave this place tomorrow and get on to the next camp, and then she would never see Étienne LeClair again. Why should the thought of him prompt her to rifle her luggage for ribbons? Nonsense. Besides, if she did have a chance to thank him for saving her, she would probably find him quite homely—not nearly so handsome as the dashing rescuer her eyes had perceived in that moment of panic.

three

"You asked to see me, sir?" Étienne stood facing Mr. Hunter before the big stone fireplace. It was too warm for him with his heavy jacket on, but he didn't dare take it off. He wished he'd thought of it before he left the kitchen.

The boss stood up and looked him over, from his oiled leather boots on up. "I understand you're the one who dredged my daughter from the pond this morning."

Étienne pulled his gaze from the eyes that pierced like a blue steel dagger. "Yes, sir."

"Well, now." Hunter's voice softened, and Étienne shot him a glance. "What's your name?"

"LeClair, sir."

Hunter's brow furrowed. "And your first name?"

"Étienne, *monsieur*." He saw doubt in the boss's eyes and added, "It means the same as Stephen."

Hunter's brow cleared. "Oh, Stephen. Why didn't you say so? Well, listen here, Steve. . .you are from Quebec?"

"Yes, sir." Étienne fought back a smile. It was well known in camp that the boss spoke next to no French, and he always pronounced the foreman's name, Robert, with a decidedly American inflection.

"You speak English well."

"Thank you, sir."

"Can you read?"

Étienne flushed. The man apparently assumed all Canadians were illiterate. "Yes, sir."

"And write?"

He nodded.

"In French?"

"Yes."

"And English?"

Étienne clenched and unclenched his fingers. How long was this to go on? "Yes, sir, I learned both."

Hunter nodded. "Good, good. And how are you with figures, boy?"

"I. . .have studied the mathematics."

"Can you figure board feet?"

He smiled then. "Oh, yes, sir."

"Can you add columns of figures?"

"Of course." He winced as he realized the boss might take that answer as rude.

Hunter reached into his vest pocket and produced a sheet of paper. "Can you tell me what this says?"

Étienne reached for it and held it toward the firelight. "It appears to be an order, sir. Five hundred board feet of oak flooring and two hundred board feet of clear pine boards."

Hunter nodded, frowning, and Étienne wondered if he had displeased him.

"Here you go, LeClair." Hunter held something out to him.

Étienne hesitated, then extended his hand, palm up, and felt the heavy weight of a coin.

He looked down at the lustrous gold disk. An American five-dollar gold piece! He swallowed hard and licked his lips, not sure what to say.

"That's a little something extra for you. Just a token of my gratitude."

"There's no need for that, sir." Étienne held the coin out toward him.

"Keep it."

"But I didn't—"

"I know. You didn't expect a reward for your service. But I daresay you can use it, eh?"

"Well. . ."

"Sure you can. Got a wife and kiddies that you send half

your pay to, back home in Quebec, have you?"

"No, sir. But there is my mother. . . ." Étienne looked down at the coin that was warming in his hand. It was true that most of the lumberjacks sent the bulk of their pay home. They spent the whole winter away from their families in hopes of earning enough to see them through to next year. If not for his widowed mother and three younger siblings still at home, Étienne would not be this far from the farm. But the wages were good here. The monthly payday made the hard work, debilitating cold, and primitive conditions worthwhile.

"There you go. She'll be proud when you send her something extra this month." Hunter clapped him on the shoulder. "It doesn't anywhere near reflect my appreciation, boy."

Étienne gulped and made himself look into the boss's eyes again. He decided Hunter was sincere, and there was no point embarrassing him by refusing his reward. "Thank you, sir."

A swish of movement at the other end of the room claimed his attention, and he caught his breath. Miss Hunter was gliding toward them across the dining hall, a vision in blue. She swept between the rough tables and smiled as she approached them. His pulse quickened. He ought to look away from her radiant face, but he couldn't.

"Well, Father, I see you've met my rescuer."

Hunter turned and stepped toward her, his eyebrows almost meeting over the bridge of his nose. "My dear, had you ought to be up so soon?"

"I'm much better, Father." She clasped his arm and flashed a smile at Étienne. "I must thank you, sir, for helping me this morning. Though I didn't say so then, I am most grateful for all you did."

Étienne felt as though all his bones had deserted him, leaving him as floppy and uncoordinated as a scarecrow. He sucked in a deep breath. "I'm glad to see you looking so well."

"I feel well," she insisted. "Might I have supper with you tonight, Father?"

"Well, yes, of course, if you don't mind forty men staring at you all the while."

Marise came in from the kitchen and began setting out the dishes for the evening meal.

"Marise," Hunter called. "Can you set a place for my daughter and me a little away from the men? Perhaps you and Robert and Steve here will join us for supper."

She inclined her head. "Of course, monsieur, but I will be serving. I am certain my husband would like to eat with you, however."

❧

Letitia felt sorry for LeClair. He sat across from her father at the table, picking at his food and fidgeting. It was obvious that he would rather be sitting elsewhere in the room, among the other men.

A twang of regret hit her. It would have pleased her if he'd acted happy to sit close to her and have a chance to further their acquaintance. Instead, he stroked his neatly trimmed beard and looked longingly toward another table where several of the fellows were chattering in French and laughing. Her French was not good enough to follow their rapid-fire banter. She almost thought she saw a flush creep up to Étienne's ears, and she wondered if the others could possibly be having fun at LeClair's expense.

She cleared her throat, and he jerked around with wide, surprised eyes.

"So, Mr. LeClair, did I hear my father say you come from Canada?"

"Oh. . .yes, mademoiselle. It is a farm close by a small village between here and Quebec City."

"I see. I expect it's much like the town where we live."

"Oh, no, I am sure it's not. It is a tiny place. You and the boss, you live in a city."

She chuckled and saw a look cross his face that made her heart skip. Was it wonder? Admiration? It certainly was not indifference. She felt a warm blush sneaking into her cheeks.

"Our town is not very large." It came out softly, and she had to look away from his eyes to regain control of her voice.

"I beg your pardon," he said. "I was mistaken."

Her father jumped in and proceeded to describe the town of Zimmerville, on the bank of the Kennebec River.

"We're near enough to bigger towns to do business," he said. "We've got the railroad and the river. That's all we need."

Once her father began talking, Letitia knew she and LeClair need not cast about for topics of interest. The boss would carry the table talk, and they need only answer an occasional question or murmur an "Mm-hmm" when appropriate.

She studied LeClair's face as he gave his attention to her father. His dark hair feathered over his forehead, where she made out a faint scar. It gave him an interesting, almost dangerous air.

She realized suddenly that she was staring at the handsome young man and looked quickly down at her plate. That was not the way a lady should behave. She picked up her knife and carefully split a biscuit down the middle.

"Will you be moving on to Round Pond Camp tomorrow, sir?" Robert asked.

To Letitia's surprise, her father hesitated. "No, I think we'll stay here one more day."

The hall was so quiet she could hear Marise clanging silverware in the kitchen.

"There are one or two things I want to accomplish," he went on, "and I think it would do my daughter good to rest another day."

Robert's expression was comical, and Letitia could almost read his mind. *Oh, no! We have to put up with the boss for another day!*

"I'm fine now, Father. Really."

He raised one hand in dismissal. "I've made up my mind. We'll stop here until Thursday. Old Guillaume tells me we may get some snow tomorrow, and if so, we'll be able to leave the wagon here and take the sled to Round Pond."

"That would be an improvement," Letitia conceded. But how would she avoid blushing every time she saw Étienne LeClair? Perhaps she would take all her meals in her room tomorrow, because she was sure that she *would* flush.

This inexplicable attraction seemed to be growing since her father had let his favor fall on LeClair. Did every woman who found herself in a perilous situation develop a fancied affection for the man who sprang to her aid? Of course, it didn't hurt that he was a muscular young man with a smile that warmed her through and through. In fact, she reflected, Étienne could probably have rescued her by simply smiling at the pond. All the ice would have melted, and she could have walked out, taken his arm, and strolled off with him in a haze of infatuation.

She glanced at him through her lowered eyelashes. LeClair concentrated on his food, as though making an effort not to look at anyone else seated near him. Again Letitia felt empathy for him. He was out of place and embarrassed to be singled out.

As if he sensed her attention, LeClair met her gaze then looked quickly away.

It struck her that she could be a major cause of his discomfiture. Unused to eating with ladies, a man of his background would consider her to be far above his station. Her presence must be excruciating for him. The only thing worse than sitting across from her would be the necessity of talking to her. She determined not to speak to him again, for his sake as well as her own.

❧

The next evening, Étienne put the checker set back in its little wooden box after soundly beating Guillaume at two games. He was tired, but the boss hadn't come into the dining hall since supper, so they'd had a relaxing evening. The men were yawning and heading for the stairs, though it was not yet eight o'clock. Work began early in the lumber camp.

He took the box of checkers and the wooden game board to the cupboard by the fireplace.

The room grew hushed, and when he turned around, he saw the cause. Mr. Hunter had come into the hall.

The boss smiled, spoke to the men nearest him, shook a few hands, and worked his way around the room. Most of the men escaped up the stairs as soon as they had greeted him.

"LeClair."

Étienne nodded. "Good evening to you, sir."

"Sit down for a moment, Steve."

Hunter smiled affably, but Étienne found it hard to smile back. Did the boss expect him to be his pal because he'd given him a five-dollar gold piece?

He tried to think of a logical reason to refuse but found none. The boss had seated himself on the bench nearest the fire, so Étienne dropped onto the one at the next table. Michael picked up his fiddle case and scurried up the stairs after the others, leaving them alone.

"How may I help you, sir?"

Hunter's smile became a grin. "I'll tell you, Steve. I suppose all the men have been wondering why I stopped here an extra day."

Étienne ran his finger along the rough edge of the table. "Well, sir, I know you were concerned about Miss Hunter's health."

"Oh, Letitia's fine. She's always had a strong constitution."

Étienne accepted that with a dubious nod.

"Not like her mother," Hunter added. "Sturdy girl. No, I had another reason."

"Sir?" Étienne croaked the word because the boss watched him closely, and he felt a response was expected.

"I stayed to watch you."

"Me?"

"You."

Étienne cleared his throat and looked about the room. Why had they all run off and left him alone with the boss?

"Sir, I assure you, when I heard Miss Hunter's cry of distress, there was nothing in my mind but—"

Hunter's laugh boomed out. "Don't be so timid, Steve! I didn't think you had designs on my daughter. That would be ridiculous."

Yes, wouldn't it? Étienne thought. The likelihood of the young lady noticing him was so remote that her father dismissed it without a further thought. But Étienne had been thinking about it for two whole days now, and little else. The very thought of Letitia Hunter looking his way was enough to set his heart romping. A woman like that—he couldn't even imagine being friends with her. And yet his brain insisted on imagining the impossible—being loved by her.

"But good has come from that incident," the boss said.

"It. . .has?" Étienne didn't like the prickly feelings that ran up his arms and down his spine.

"Yes, indeed! You see, it brought you to my notice." Hunter leaned toward him and smiled. "I guess you've seen me watching you the last couple of days?"

"I—" Étienne gulped. He had felt the boss's eyes on him more than once and tried his best to stay out of Hunter's line of vision.

"Well, I like to learn a little bit about a man before I do business with him."

What on earth? Étienne sent up a quick prayer. *Lord, please give me Your peace. This man is driving me insane with all this talk. If he's going to fire me, please let him be quick about it.*

Hunter sat back and scrutinized him with those penetrating blue eyes. "I've seen for myself that you're strong and diligent. No slouch mentally, either. And the other men like you. Robert has told me you are trustworthy. In fact, I understand that yesterday after rescuing my daughter, you were entrusted with a sum of money and drove to town for supplies."

"*C'est vrai*, monsieur." Étienne winced. He had intended not to lapse into French. "I mean, that is the truth."

Hunter nodded. "Well, Steve, it's like this: I'd like to offer you a position in my office."

Everything stopped then as Étienne stared at him. "Sir?"

"My office, back in Zimmerville. I'd like to take you back there with me. My head clerk is retiring, and I have a spot for a bright young fellow like you."

Étienne looked away, his heart racing. "I. . .don't know what to say, sir. What does the job entail?"

"Just what I've asked you about. Writing letters, making up orders and invoices, keeping accounts. . ."

"I. . .might need some direction, sir."

"You shall have it. I'll ask Mr. Weston to stay on and train you."

Étienne hesitated, not wanting to ask, but not wanting to agree, either, until he knew a few things. Hunter was watching him, so he inhaled and dove in. "And the pay, sir? If I may ask."

"The same as you're getting now, but a lot easier work. If you do well, I shall raise it a dollar a week this summer."

Fragments of thoughts raced through Étienne's mind. The same pay, but with a softer life. He would be in an office all day, not out in the fresh air. Would he suffocate? It was a hard life in the lumber camps, working all day in the bitter cold, and dangerous, too. He'd seen several men killed or maimed while logging. But he doubted many men died while keeping accounts.

Of course, he would not get to go home in the summer, as he did now. His mother wouldn't like that, and he would miss his younger brothers and sisters terribly, but if he could help them more, help them have a better life. . .

He would live in a town. He'd never done that before. His family scraped out a life on a small, stony farm. The nearest village had only a church and one small shop that was really a widow's parlor stocked with basic merchandise. He thought he might like to live in a real town, at least for a while. Maybe there would be a library there, or a shop that sold books.

And a bit more pay in the summer. That sounded good. Surely by then he'd be able to send more home to his family. Of course, there would be no bunkhouse in the city.

"Well?" Hunter's bushy eyebrows nearly met, he was frowning so.

"What about housing, sir?"

"Of course you'd have to board somewhere."

Étienne's hopes plummeted. "Well, sir, I don't think. . ."

Hunter shook his head. "Yes, yes, I see. All right, I'll cut you a housing allowance. Not much, you understand."

"Of course."

"There's quite a French quarter in the town. I expect you can find a place to board among them."

"That would be. . .agreeable, sir."

"So you're accepting my offer?"

"I. . .yes."

It was done. He had committed himself to work in the lumber company office. At once he wondered if he was making a mistake. But he wouldn't have to stay there forever. If he hated it, he would work for six months or a year, then resign and go back to Quebec.

At that moment, Letitia Hunter came into the room, and they both stood. Etienne's pulse picked up, and he tried not to stare at her.

"Letitia! I thought you'd retired." Her father smiled, and Étienne was glad. A man who loved his child had some tenderness, some compassion.

"I'm just about to, Father. I wanted to ask you to wake me when you get up in the morning so that I don't delay the trip. With this snow and the warmer temperatures, we should have a pleasant journey to Round Pond."

"Steve here is coming with us tomorrow," Hunter said.

Letitia blinked up at her father, and her cheeks flushed. "He is driving us to the next camp?"

"And all the way back to the depot in Bangor. He's going to replace Weston in the office."

Letitia turned to stare at him; then her lips parted. She dropped her gaze after a moment, and the flush was undeniable. Étienne wondered what she was thinking.

"That is. . .good news." She stepped toward him and extended her hand. "I'm pleased, Mr. LeClair. Father has been telling me these two years he would hire another clerk. And now, with Mr. Weston finishing his tenure and business increasing, we are getting desperate. You are most welcome."

Étienne took her small, soft hand in his for an instant. Its warmth surprised and thrilled him. So different from when he'd pulled her from the icy pond.

"Mademoiselle is looking well," he said. "I am glad you have recovered from your accident."

"Thank you. And now, good night, gentlemen. I shall see you at breakfast."

Étienne watched her go, with her brown woolen skirt swaying gracefully about her as she walked. He felt the boss watching him and quickly shifted his gaze. No good. How would he ever keep from staring at her on the long trip tomorrow?

four

The sleigh sped over the trail toward Round Pond, gliding on the new snow. Three inches had fallen in the night—not much, but enough to ease their journey and the work of the lumberjacks.

Lincoln Hunter insisted on driving the first stretch, and Letitia sat beside him. The sun rose as they left Spruce Run, sending its rays down through the frosted branches to sparkle off the pristine snow. The air was warmer than it had been for several days. The only thing that marred the excursion was her constant awareness of Étienne LeClair, sitting behind them with the bags and bundles.

He remained silent throughout the first two hours, and Letitia had to force herself not to look back to be sure he was still with them. How would she ever keep from watching him in Zimmerville, where they would be working in the same room every day? It promised to be awkward. What was her father thinking, bringing such a handsome and likable young man into the office?

Under other circumstances, she would have looked forward to becoming acquainted with Étienne. Their few attempts at conversation intrigued her. He seemed intelligent and thoughtful. Surely they could find some common ground. Since she'd begun working full time, she'd lost contact with most of her friends, and she missed having other young people to talk to. Étienne could fill that gap, in a different situation.

But her father would never sanction a friendship between her and his clerk. She practiced cordiality to all the employees of Northern Lumber in Zimmerville, but her father had made it clear that she was not to socialize with them. The one exception was her friendship with the lumberyard foreman, Jacques Laplante, and his wife, Angelique. Her father tolerated some interaction with the family, but then, he didn't know the extent of her relationship with the Laplantes. And a foreman was a foreman, after all. A clerk, however. . . No, Father would never countenance an affinity between his daughter and a clerk.

Instead of dwelling on her new coworker, she made small talk with her father about business—the quality of the wood his crews were producing and the likelihood of more snow to make hauling the logs to the rivers and railroads easier.

She thought he looked tired, and she was glad their circuit of the camps would soon end. His face seemed a little off color, and the lines at the corners of his mouth were more pronounced these days.

The horses slowed, and he leaned forward, squinting down the path of unbroken snow ahead of them.

"Something's in the road."

A stirring behind her focused Letitia's awareness on LeClair once more as she shaded her eyes to look ahead.

"There's a tree down, sir."

Letitia jumped. The young Frenchman's voice was very close to her, and his warm breath tickled her cheek.

Her father guided the team up close to the obstacle and halted them. Letitia stared at the huge tamarack lying in the roadway.

"Well." Her father sighed.

The sleigh frame creaked and shivered, and Letitia turned to see that LeClair had sprung out and now rummaged among the bundles. He produced an ax and advanced on the fallen tree without waiting for instruction.

Her father sank back in the seat. "Well, I'm glad we have a strong man along. If I'd been out here alone with Weston, we'd have been all day making a way past that."

Letitia felt a flush of gladness at LeClair's willingness to help out. She sneaked a glance in her father's direction, wondering if he felt poorly. In the past, she would have expected him to be the one to jump out and attack the tree trunk.

The lumberjack walked along the tree, from one side of the roadway to the other, looking it over, then climbed on it near the smaller end and began to swing his axe. Under his firm, rapid blows, limbs soon began to fall from the trunk, exposing the log. LeClair set his feet again and began to chop with rhythmic, powerful swings.

Letitia stirred and laid aside the traveling robe.

"What are you doing?" her father asked.

"I am going to help him. I can't do much, but perhaps I can drag aside the limbs he's cut off."

"Stay here."

Her father rose and began to clamber out of the sled.

"Father, you should rest. You've driven for two hours and you're tired."

"Nonsense."

Letitia gathered her skirts and climbed down on her side. If he could be stubborn, so could she.

Her father grasped the end of a large branch that lay between the team and the fallen tree. Letitia took hold of a smaller one and followed him, dragging her burden through the loose snow to one side. It was harder than she'd expected.

She and her father both stood panting when they'd finished. He looked as though he were about to speak sharply, so she hastened to haul away another, smaller limb. When she had disposed of it, her father had made his way closer to where LeClair stood on the log, chopping.

"Hey, Steve!"

The ax froze in midair.

"Sir?"

"What's the plan?"

LeClair straightened and rested his ax with the head against his boot. "Well, sir, I thought I'd leave some stumps of the branches and hitch the team to them. They ought to be able to pull that end of the tree off the road, and we'll be able to get around the bigger part. I haven't left any more than I had to, and I think they'll be able to haul that smaller end away. If they can't, I'll have to chop that part into shorter lengths. It could take some time, sir."

"How can I help?" Letitia asked.

"I think you've done all you can for now, mademoiselle. It's just a matter of my chopping on through the trunk." He smiled and lifted the ax again, hefting it between his hands as though eager to get on with the job. Letitia caught her breath. There was something in his gaze that made her feel alive and happy she had met him.

Hunter nodded and stepped back. "Sounds good to me. I guess you'd better have at it."

They sat in the sleigh, watching him. After a few minutes, LeClair unbuttoned his thick wool jacket and removed it, tossing it behind him among the tamarack limbs. He renewed his efforts, and Letitia watched speechless. His every move was purposeful but graceful. The chips flew as he raised the ax again and again, putting his considerable strength behind each blow.

She had never watched a man work so hard before. As a girl, she'd been sheltered from such scenes. Now that she worked in the office, she often saw laborers loading lumber and moving logs in the lumberyard, but it wasn't a steady, driving force like this. She wondered at his stamina and the beauty of his effort.

"Are you sure he's worth as much in the office?" she asked softly. The idea of caging Étienne LeClair seemed almost cruel, now that she'd seen his skill in the outdoors.

Her father had sunk back against the seat, his eyes closed. Alarmed, she leaned toward him and shook his arm.

"Father, are you all right?"

He jumped and opened his eyes. "What? Oh, yes, yes, I'm fine. Didn't sleep well last night."

"Are you sure you're not ill?"

He sat up straighter. "No, I'm not ill. But the meal we had last night didn't agree with me."

"The moose meat in the stew was tender," she said.

"Yes, I've nothing against moose meat. But the beans. . ."

Letitia hid a smile. When her mother was alive, he had forbidden her to ever let the cook serve dry beans, whether baked, stewed, or otherwise. Mrs. Watkins remembered, and beans never graced the table in the Hunter home.

"Well, you didn't have to eat them."

Étienne leaped down from the log and rested his ax against it.

Letitia rose. "You stay here, Father."

"I will not."

She sighed and hurried to help Étienne, who was clearing away a few more severed limbs. As he turned toward her, she could feel the warmth radiating from him, and his dark hair clung to his damp forehead. His eyes, as before, inspired confidence in her. It was like the day he pulled her from the pond; he was capable of putting all things right for her.

Without considering the propriety of it, she blurted, "I'm worried about Father, Mr. LeClair."

He frowned, and his gaze flickered past her for a moment.

"The boss is ill?"

"He says he's not, but. . ."

Étienne nodded. "Come, we can get this. Can you hold the horses' heads while I unhitch the whiffletree?"

"Here, Steve, wait for me!" Her father puffed a little as he plodded toward them.

"I think that your help is not required, monsieur." Étienne smiled at her father and walked to where the harness was hitched to the whiffletree, between the team and the sleigh.

Letitia approached the nearest horse and gingerly reached out to stroke the huge animal's nose. The horse snorted and shook his head, then stretched his neck toward her. She gasped, then laughed and scratched his forelock.

"Just hold still, you overgrown puppy."

She took hold of the cheek strap, knowing that if the big Belgian decided to move, she wouldn't be able to stop him. But the team stood patiently while Étienne unhitched the harness from the sled.

He gathered the reins and called, "Now, mademoiselle. Release them."

Letitia stepped back, and Étienne lifted the reins and clucked. The two horses moved forward, and he maneuvered them to a spot in front of the log, turning them with the ease of an experienced driver.

"That Steve's a good man," her father said.

"Yes, he is. Are you sure he wouldn't make a good foreman at one of the lumber camps?"

"He probably would. But right now I need a clerk, and he speaks French."

"What has that to do with anything?"

Her father watched Étienne attach a chain from the whiffletree around the stubs of branches on the log.

"You know we're doing business with the shingle mills in Quebec. If I've got somebody who speaks the language, I'll feel a lot better placing orders with them. I might even send him up there one day to look things over for me and make sure they're not shorting me on my orders."

Letitia nodded. Last fall her father had blustered for weeks before finally placing a large order with a Canadian mill. He'd prefer an American company but couldn't find one that produced the volume of cedar shingles his clients demanded.

"Are you still considering opening a shingle mill in Fairfield?" she asked.

"Thinking on it."

Étienne hopped over the fallen tree and stood on the other side with the reins in his hands. He clucked to the horses, and they leaned into their collars. At first the log didn't move, but he called quietly to them, his French words soft and sweet.

Letitia wished she knew what promises he crooned to them.

The tree shivered and began to move. The team gained momentum, pulling the smaller half down the road, past the sleigh and off to one side.

"I'm going to help him." Letitia ran down the path the log had carved in the snow, reaching Étienne as he fumbled to unhitch the team. He straightened and grinned at her.

"Bien, mademoiselle. You can hold the reins for me, yes?"

She took them, feeling happy and hopeful as his bright smile warmed her. He removed his gloves and unfastened the chains, then let the whiffletree rest on the ground.

"Thank you." He reached for the reins.

"You're welcome."

She walked with him behind the huge horses and again held the reins while he hooked the team to the sleigh. Her cheeks must be scarlet, but perhaps it was only because of her small exertion and the crisp air. She sent up a quick prayer of thanks that they'd had such a strong and capable man along in this small crisis.

"Father, perhaps Mr. LeClair should drive now," she said. "I'll sit behind, and you can rest."

"I'm all right."

She clamped her lips tight. Her father was becoming irritated, and she mustn't imply any further that he wasn't fit.

"Fine. Drive if you want, but I'd like to close my eyes for a little while, and I thought I'd curl up in the back." She held out her hand to LeClair, and he assisted her as she climbed into the back compartment of the sleigh and settled among the bundles. She poked about and found her pillow. When she turned toward the front, LeClair held out the robe she'd tucked over her legs for the first part of the trip.

"Mademoiselle," he murmured.

"Oh, thank you. You might want it, though."

"It is warm now. I shall not need it." He retrieved his jacket and ax, placing the ax in the bed of the sleigh with her and his coat on the front seat, between her father and the empty spot where he would sit. Looking toward her father, he said, "Would you allow me to guide the team for you, sir?"

Letitia thought he chose each word carefully and pronounced it with precision, with as little accent as possible. Or perhaps for Étienne, it was with an accent—an American-English accent. He had it almost perfect when he spoke slowly. How many other things was he doing, without her even noticing, to please her father?

It unsettled her somehow, to think of him in a servile position. As a lumberjack, he was an employee, but he had his freedom. As her father's clerk, he would be at the beck and call of a moody man every minute of every workday. Could he stand that? Letitia could barely stand it herself, and the boss was her father.

Yet LeClair seemed to understand what he had gotten himself into when he accepted the job and was studying how to stay in the boss's favor. Was it purely for his own advancement, or did he truly want to do a good job for Northern Lumber? And how long would it last? She would observe his adjustment to his new duties with interest.

❧

They pulled into the camp at Round Pond late that evening. Étienne unloaded the sleigh, then unharnessed the horses and put them away for the night. By the time he entered the bunkhouse, the boss and his daughter had been shown to their quarters.

Round Pond Camp was larger and more civilized than Spruce Run, and the Hunters were given a small cabin a short distance from the bunkhouse. Étienne found a plate of beans and biscuits awaiting him in the kitchen and was then directed upstairs to an empty bunk. He pulled off his boots and sank onto the mattress with only time enough for a brief, silent prayer of thanks before he fell asleep.

In the morning, he rose with the other workmen before

dawn and was pleased to find two, Marc and Adrian, with whom he had worked the winter before.

"You are taking the boss to the train?" Marc asked.

"*Oui*, and I am going to work in his office, doing paperwork for him."

The two stared at him. "This is unthinkable," Adrian said in French.

"Why?" Étienne laughed. "You think I cannot learn something new?"

"No, but. . ."

Marc clapped him on the shoulder. "You will die of boredom, my friend. You are not a man who will like to live in the city and do every minute what the boss asks you to do."

"He will eat you alive before spring," Adrian predicted.

Marc nodded. "His temper can be foul, they say."

A shadow of apprehension fell on Étienne, dulling his customary good humor. "I have also heard this, but I have not seen him angry. He is traveling with his daughter, and perhaps she is a good influence."

"Oh, that is why you are doing this." Adrian laughed.

"She is pretty, no?" Marc asked. "I have been told she is a beauty, but me, I have not seen her."

They went down to breakfast together, and Étienne was relieved when the cook informed him that the boss and Miss Hunter were taking breakfast in their cabin. He was to meet them in an hour.

He spent the morning touring the camp and the logging sites nearby with Mr. Hunter. After lunch, the boss went over some records with the foreman and had Étienne copy statistics on dozens of aspects of the operation: hours spent on various tasks, money paid out for supplies, man-hours lost to accidents and illness, number of board feet of various species of wood originating from the Round Pond Camp, and even the number of times the traveling doctor and preacher had visited the men. Then Mr. Hunter dictated two letters, which Étienne took down in carefully scripted English. He was glad Miss Hunter was not in the room, or he would never have been able to keep his attention on the meticulous work. But the boss looked the letters over afterward and nodded his approval, much to Étienne's relief. Perhaps this assignment would not be so difficult.

At the supper table that evening, the other men reopened the topic of the boss's daughter, to Étienne's consternation. Several of them reported seeing her that day from a distance, and an argument arose as to whether or not she was beautiful.

"I saw her last night," said Richard, who had helped Étienne stable the horses. "It is hard to tell much about a person all bundled up in cloaks and bonnets. But her face, what I saw of it? Yes, *très jolie*. Very pretty."

The other men laughed, and Adrian said, "Ask Étienne if she is pretty. You have seen her up close, have you not?"

Étienne felt his face go crimson and was glad he still had his beard. He would shave once their traveling ended; he was sure the boss would want him to come to the office well groomed. But for now, the beard not only kept him warm but also hid his embarrassment.

"You ought not to speak so lightly of the boss's daughter," he said, but this only brought more laughter.

How could he make them understand that, though Letitia Hunter was indeed a lovely woman, she should not be the object of their jesting? They meant no harm, but still, it made him uncomfortable.

They all vowed they envied him, but he reflected that it was not necessarily a good thing to be thrown into close association with a lady. The past two days had been a trial for him as he strove to keep a courteous demeanor in her presence. Most of the time, he tried not to look at her unless circumstances demanded it. If he did look her way, she might see his growing admiration for her, or worse yet, her father would. And if one thing would anger the boss, that would be it.

five

Two things brought great relief to Étienne when they stepped off the train in Zimmerville the next night. The first was the large, hearty man who met them, welcoming the boss and Miss Hunter like old friends.

He was French. Étienne tried not to show his surprise when Mr. Hunter introduced the middle-aged man as the lumberyard foreman, Jack Laplante. With him was another man, René Ouellette, younger and definitely less at ease around the boss.

The second thing was the revelation that Étienne would separate from the Hunters almost immediately.

"You will stay with René and his family." Laplante grinned and slapped Étienne's shoulder. "You will find that René's wife, Sophie, is a wonderful cook. The good luck has found you today, my friend."

The boss had sent a telegram from the railroad station in Bangor, and apparently Laplante had made this arrangement with Ouellette, who worked in the sawmill. Étienne was glad. René smiled at him when the boss wasn't looking. The young man seemed a bit timid but sprang to gather the Hunters' baggage and stow it in a carriage. Laplante instructed Étienne to go with René to his new quarters.

Étienne hesitated and looked toward the boss.

"Go on, Steve," Hunter said. "You've done well on this journey, but we'll let Jack take over now and see us safely home. You go and get settled. Oh, and bring those papers with you tomorrow. Ouellette can show you where the office is when he comes to the mill."

"Yes, sir."

Hunter turned and sought out his daughter. "Ready, Letitia?"

"Yes, Father." Before she followed Hunter, she threw a quick glance toward Étienne. He smiled and nodded, wondering when he would see her again. She returned his nod and stepped forward to allow Laplante to assist her into the carriage.

René insisted on carrying Étienne's small bag on the quarter-mile walk from the station to his home, but Étienne kept the leather writing case the boss had entrusted to him tucked firmly under his arm.

When he'd first received the case, he'd hesitated to touch the papers already inside, but Hunter had encouraged him to study them and copy the way the records were compiled at the other camps. At that point, Étienne had wondered if the boss had written them himself, but the neat, dainty script belied that. Had there been another clerk on the first part of Hunter's journey?

The tiny initials at the bottom of each page had not registered until he'd opened the case once more on the train to review his paperwork. *L.H.* The boss's initials, yet. . . Was it possible the boss's daughter had recorded the statistics for her father until they reached Spruce Run? He wanted to ask but didn't dare.

She'd kept her distance from him, so far as possible while traveling together. She was polite and even smiled at him now and then, but it was a cool smile, not like the one she had given him when she'd held the horses for him on the road.

They were in her world now, and he suspected he would see very little of her. If they did meet again, he must not assume she would treat him as anything other than her father's man.

René Ouellette loosened up when they were away from the train depot and the boss's eye. "My wife and I are pleased that you are willing to stay with us, Monsieur LeClair. Our home is small, and with four children it is crowded and sometimes noisy. But I do hope you will find it to your liking."

"I'm sure it will be fine," Étienne said. "But are you certain you can spare the room?"

"Well, monsieur, the truth is, Sophie and I could use the extra income your board would bring. My wife, she used to do sewing for people, but with the last baby, it was too much for her. So when Jacques came to the sawmill this afternoon and told me a place was needed for the new clerk, I went home and asked Sophie. She agreed. We can put the three girls all in one room, and you shall have the front upstairs. It is small, but. . ." René shrugged and watched him anxiously.

"It sounds ideal," Étienne assured him. "But you must call me by my given name."

"But monsieur is to work in the office."

"That makes no difference. I'm a poor fellow from eastern Quebec, and I'm no better than you. Please call me Étienne."

By the time they reached the little house, Étienne felt he had made a new friend. The children were in bed, but Sophie greeted them and showed him up the narrow stairs with a candle.

"This is the room, monsieur. It is tiny, I know." She stood back from the doorway.

Étienne ducked as he passed through the low doorway and looked around. The cot was freshly made up with a cheerful patchwork quilt, and a stool and small table sat beneath the window. Pegs on the wall would easily hold his few clothes.

"I used to share a room about this size with my three brothers. It is perfect, madame."

Sophie smiled and assured him that the price he offered was agreeable. She knew he was tired. Her husband would bring him a pitcher of water and answer any questions he had.

Twenty minutes later, Étienne blew out his candle and lay back on the cot, weary but content. The specter of the office loomed in the darkness, but he refused to be intimidated by that. He rolled on his side and looked toward the small window. He could see a cluster of stars. This chamber would be more comfortable than a bunk at one of the lumber camps in a room with forty other men. God had worked this out for him so effortlessly. Surely the office was nothing to be feared.

❧

The next morning, Letitia was travel weary; her stiff, sore muscles pained her when she climbed out of bed.

Mrs. Watkins, the cook, had left sliced ham and fresh eggs in the icebox, and the scent of coffee filled the warm kitchen. In the bread box, Letitia found biscuits and oatmeal bread. As usual, she prepared breakfast, knowing Mrs. Watkins would come in later to fix luncheon and dinner.

She was beginning to wonder if her father had overslept when he came into the dining room yawning. His eyes were rimmed below with dark smudges, and she felt a pang of anxiety.

"Are you sure you ought to go to the office today, Father?"

"What kind of nonsense is that? Of course I'm going in."

"You've had a strenuous trip. Mr. Weston can—"

"Mr. Weston knows how I like to run things." Her father's stern tone silenced Letitia. "As if I would turn up late on the first day of LeClair's employment. What kind of example would that set him? As to Mr. Weston, I expect he'll be on time, don't you?"

"Well, of course."

"Of course," her father agreed. "He has never been late in the thirty years he's worked for me, and I presume he won't be during the last two weeks of his employment. After that, I expect you and LeClair to continue the custom of punctuality we hold to at Northern Lumber."

Letitia looked down at her plate. "Yes, Father." It was no use to hint that he needed more rest. Lincoln Hunter was not a man to rest when his employees were working. Suggesting that his stamina was flagging would only bring his displeasure.

When they arrived, Weston had already unlocked the office and started a fire in the stove and was showing Étienne LeClair his new desk.

"I shall stay on another fortnight to assist you, Mr. LeClair, so in the interim—" Weston broke off as Letitia and her father entered. "Ah, Mr. Hunter."

"Morning, Weston. LeClair." Lincoln Hunter nodded at the two men and strode toward his large walnut desk at the far end of the room.

Letitia stepped inside and met LeClair's stunned gaze. Obviously he had not anticipated seeing her here. She noticed then that he had shaved. His brown hair fell thick and shiny over his brow, and his firm jaw was the perfect complement to his huge brown eyes. He wore a red plaid flannel shirt, which seemed out of place in the office, but she supposed he hadn't had a chance to purchase anything else. It brought a rugged, masculine air to the usually subdued room.

She hesitated, feeling a flush work its way up her neck as their gazes locked. Father hadn't told him, then. He must have thought she only took the trip for entertainment. She decided to let Weston explain her situation to him. Smiling in their direction, she glided toward her desk with a brisk, "Good morning. Hello, Mr. Weston."

"Welcome back, Miss Letitia."

"Thank you." If only her cheeks didn't go scarlet whenever she was near Étienne. This couldn't go on. She would get used to him, and soon it would be a mundane thing to enter a room and find a fine-looking lumberjack there. She was sure she could train her pulse not to hammer so violently in his presence.

LeClair cleared his throat. He opened his mouth, but closed it without saying anything and nodded.

She turned her back to the men and hung up her cloak and bonnet. Weston's quiet voice went on, explaining to LeClair that he wanted him to take over the head clerk's desk immediately.

"I will be nearby to explain anything you need help with, but I do think it's best if you take charge of the orders and correspondence right away."

"But, sir—" Étienne paused, then murmured, "As you wish, Mr. Weston."

"Very good. And if you are quick, why, then you won't need me as long as Mr. Hunter seems to think you will."

Letitia sat down and drew a stack of papers toward her. She knew Weston had done the banking and urgent accounts during her absence, but a backlog of bills to be paid had accumulated and several orders and payments needed to be posted to the ledger.

Weston began his lesson with LeClair. "Now, we had this order come in yesterday for lumber and shingles. It's from a private individual, not a contractor. I'll show you how we write it up for the lumberyard foreman. You've met Mr. Laplante?"

"Yes, sir."

Letitia couldn't help looking over at them. Her desk was situated with one end against the wall halfway along the room. Her father's lair was behind her, and Weston's desk— now LeClair's—sat at the other end, facing the window. She had grown accustomed to seeing Weston's back all day as he bent over his work. She'd often wondered why he faced the wall and window, not the room, and had decided he disliked being distracted. When customers entered, they usually went straight to Mr. Hunter's desk or stopped to inquire of Letitia about their business. Apparently Mr. Weston liked it that way, but perhaps the young Frenchman would rather turn the desk around and face the room. But if he did that, how would she keep from staring at him? She concluded that the desk being turned the other way was a good thing.

LeClair was much larger than the elderly clerk, and when he sat in the oak chair before the desk, his bulk blocked a great deal of light from the window. He seemed too big for the desk, in fact, for the room. In spite of his quiet manner, he brought a vitality into the office that made Letitia want to shout and laugh.

Weston pulled one of the chairs usually reserved for clients over nearer Étienne's desk. He instructed the younger man in quiet tones on where to find the record books, loose paper, envelopes, and other items necessary for the job. Then he told him to take a fresh sheet of paper and prepare the order for the foreman. Letitia noted that Weston did nothing but sit with his hands folded and talk to LeClair, making the younger man think about each task and do it unassisted.

She made herself concentrate on her own work, and for the next half hour all remained quiet.

"Weston!" her father suddenly bellowed, and she jumped.

Weston turned toward the boss. "Yes, sir?"

"I've been going through this mail, and I need you to take a letter."

"Very good, sir. I'm sure Mr. LeClair can accommodate you."

"Hmph," was all that came from Lincoln Hunter's corner, and Letitia smiled to herself. Weston had always had a way of keeping her father in line, like a tutor instructing a naughty schoolboy. She would miss the old man.

Étienne rose slowly.

"Take your pen and paper," Weston said softly, "and the portable desk to write on."

Étienne gathered the supplies, fumbling a bit as he hurried. Letitia thought as he turned from his desk that she detected a slight glint of panic in his eyes. She lowered her gaze and busied herself while he went to do her father's bidding.

Was this the way it would be from now on? Two people who hardly dared look at each other working in the same room all day?

She thought much about the matter that first day, and in the days that followed. Étienne kept his place, never leaving his desk unless his job demanded it, never speaking to her unless it pertained to business.

Under the eyes of both her father and Mr. Weston, Letitia felt both men stifled the natural inclination to talk and become acquainted. But her father liked a quiet, professional office, and

Mr. Weston knew that well. The influence of the two of them dulled any inclination she might feel to liven things up. She was a clerk, and she must keep her demeanor in line with her position. Étienne certainly did, and she respected him for that. She wouldn't want to embarrass him or risk causing unwanted attention to fall his way.

Still, she found she liked him more and more. Was he ignoring her only to avoid her father's displeasure, or had he decided he didn't like her well enough to take the risk? He didn't seem frightened of her father, but respectful and perhaps a bit wary. She knew Étienne had seen the boss's irritable side when a customer failed to pay his outstanding bill. But was that the only reason he kept away from her, or had her own aloofness put him off? He must be lonely, so far from his family and friends. Letitia was lonely, too.

By the end of Mr. Weston's tenure, she longed to talk to Étienne and learn more about him. She saw his face brighten whenever Jacques Laplante entered the office, and she inferred that they were now friends. She wondered if they saw each other after-hours.

She determined on the second Sunday after they returned from the trip north that she would visit the Laplantes after church and see if she could coax some information from Angelique without seeming nosy.

Her father slept late on Sunday, the one day of the week that he indulged himself. Although it grieved Letitia that he no longer went to church since her mother died, she was glad he was at least getting some rest. He still looked a bit run-down to her.

She'd brought up the subject of church a few times, hoping he would attend with her, but he dismissed it brashly. So she went alone. If he asked her later how the service was—which was rare—she would give him an honest but vague answer. At this point, it seemed better not to divulge to him that she had quit attending the large, traditional church the Hunters had belonged to for years. Instead, at Angelique Laplante's invitation, she now went to the smaller, less ostentatious church the Laplantes attended on the edge of town.

She entered the little church just a minute or two before the service was scheduled to begin and looked toward the pew where Jacques, Angelique, and their children always sat.

Letitia stopped short in the aisle. Someone else was sitting with the Laplantes, and the pew was so full she doubted it would hold her as well. Was it their son-in-law? No, the man sitting between Jacques and fifteen-year-old Matthieu was broader through the shoulders than Marie's husband. In fact, that straight back and wavy, dark hair looked suspiciously like...

He turned his head slightly, and she caught her breath. Étienne LeClair was sitting with the Laplantes. And wearing a suit. Of course, he had received his first pay envelope on Friday. The coat fit flawlessly over his muscular shoulders and suited him as well as his casual work clothes.

She slipped into a pew near the back and hoped Angelique would not spot her before the service began. She couldn't fit in the row with them all if she wanted to, and she certainly didn't want to force a situation where Étienne would have to converse with her in public. That might embarrass him, and it might also start tongues wagging.

As they sang the opening anthem, her galloping pulse slowed. Why was she so tense over Étienne's appearance at church? She ought to rejoice. Did he share her faith, or had he come to please his new friends?

When the service ended, she made her way without haste to the front door. Without lingering, she walked leisurely toward the street.

"Miss Letitia! Wait!"

She turned and smiled at Angelique. "Hello."

"I did not see you before. I was afraid you were sick."

Letitia shook her head. "I saw that your pew was full, so I sat farther back."

"Ah." Angelique leaned closer. "Did you see? Étienne, the new clerk, he came with us today."

"Yes, I saw. That's wonderful."

"He is boarding with the Ouellettes, you know."

"I heard."

"Sophie Ouellette is very glad to have him. She says he is the perfect boarder—neat and quiet, doesn't go out to drink at night, and he gets along well with the little ones. He told her he has younger brothers at home, so he is used to children."

"I'm glad they are getting on so well."

Angelique nodded. "But they go to the big church—you know. Étienne went with them last week, but he told my husband it was not the same as what he was used to and he felt lost in that crowd. So Jacques, he said, 'Why don't you try our little church?' And, *voilà*! He is here."

Letitia smiled. "Did he like it?"

"I think so, yes. He is eating dinner with us now, and I will ask him this question."

Angelique's youngest daughter, seven-year-old Colette, joined them and grasped Letitia's hand. "Mademoiselle, are you coming to our house today?"

"Oh, I think not," Letitia said with a pang of regret. "You have other company. Perhaps next week."

Angelique straightened her shoulders. "You must not stay away because of the new clerk."

Letitia bit her lip, trying to sort the feelings at war inside her. "Yes, dear friend, I think I must. He would be embarrassed, you see, if I came today. He is new here, and he didn't know he would be working with me every day, and I'm sure he's glad on Sunday to be away from my father and me. This is his time not to have to think about the office, but if I am there. . ."

Disappointment registered on both faces. "Perhaps you are right," Angelique said. "But next week you must come, and I will not invite Étienne. But after he is settled here and things are not so. . ."

"So silly," said Colette, and Letitia smiled.

"I was thinking so complicated," her mother corrected. "Then at that time, we shall invite you both."

"Oh, no, you really shouldn't." Letitia glanced toward the church door and saw Jacques and Étienne speaking with the pastor.

"I shouldn't?"

"No. If Father heard, he would not understand, and I don't think—"

Étienne was about to descend the church steps. He glanced her way and froze for an instant. His eyes lit, and his lips twitched as though a smile were struggling to escape.

Letitia swallowed hard and tried to inhale without gasping.

Angelique nodded soberly, then smiled. "I see."

six

Letitia bent over her desk, concentrating on the column of figures she was adding. As March had now arrived, she was going over the figures for the previous month, as she always did. At the far end of the office, her father leaned back in his swivel chair, discussing a large order with a local contractor. John Rawley had bid successfully on building a new courthouse for the county, and while the foundation and facade would be of stone, his lumber needs would be extensive.

Dry, planed spruce from the north of Maine was selected for the framework. Walnut would be brought by ship from Pennsylvania for the wainscoting and interior details. Maine red oak would be used for the stair treads. Her father and Rawley talked on, laying out a delivery schedule for the thousands of board feet of lumber that would be needed.

Letitia was used to mentally blocking out her father's business conversations while she worked. At first she had found it an annoying distraction, but she had taught herself to go on with her calculations while the voices droned on.

"Steve!" Hunter called, and Étienne laid aside the correspondence he was working on and rose to answer the boss's summons.

A month had passed since Étienne began working in the office, and Letitia was acclimating to the presence of the quiet Canadian. The office still seemed smaller when Étienne was in it, and even though he'd bought a conservative black worsted suit, he still carried himself like an active outdoorsman. Could he be happy cooped up in here day after day? Did he regret giving up his life in the woods?

Étienne was determined to excel, she could see that, and he appeared to have conquered his nerves. He'd advanced quickly during Oscar Weston's two weeks' mentoring, and he worked mostly on his own now, tending to all the correspondence, orders, and shipping, while Letitia handled the bookkeeping and payroll.

She'd heard her father bragging about LeClair yesterday to one of his friends while Étienne was out of the office. "He's worth twice as much in the office as he was in the woods," he'd said. She wondered about that, knowing Étienne's skill with an ax. But if her father believed that, why hadn't he raised the clerk's salary to equal what he'd paid Mr. Weston?

The small central Maine city of Zimmerville, where the office and lumber mill were located, had a high percentage of Canadian transplants. Already Hunter relied heavily on LeClair for dealing with French-speaking clients, for interviewing prospective workers who spoke no English, and for correspondence with business contacts in Quebec. He also entrusted more and more details of the technical side of the business to the young man. But Hunter insisted on using the anglicized form of the clerk's name and had no dealings with him outside the office.

Rawley's laugh reached her, and Letitia frowned. The contractor was not one of her favorite customers. When he visited the office, he always made a point of speaking to her in a manner she found far too familiar. Her reaction was to ignore him unless forced to speak to him about business.

She went on with reconciling the records for sales, wages, and expenses for the month of February. Étienne stood near her father's desk, telling him and Rawley where they could best obtain each of the materials on Rawley's list. He would draft letters to dealers in other areas for those not available locally. When Rawley had approved the list of materials to be ordered, it would come to Letitia; she would itemize the bill, finding the current prices and figuring the final cost. With this project,

Rawley's account promised to be one of the company's most profitable.

"We'll have the walnut shipped directly to your site," LeClair said. "The spruce and oak we'll mill here and send down the river."

Rawley discussed at length the quality he wanted to see in the lumber for the courthouse, and Letitia sneaked a glance at Étienne. He listened carefully to both men and assented to Rawley's demands and Hunter's instructions. She was proud of him. He had taken on a professional demeanor easily, even though he kept that rugged, wild essence. Already men liked to deal with him, showing confidence in his judgment.

Twenty minutes later, Étienne was dismissed, and he went quietly back to his desk. Rawley and Hunter stood up and shook hands.

"Thank you for your business," Hunter said.

"I know Northern Lumber will get everything I need, and at a decent price." Rawley pulled out his pocket watch. "Won't you and Miss Hunter join me for luncheon?"

Letitia sat still for a moment, then made herself go on writing while she waited, as if unhearing, for her father's reply. She had planned to go home, as usual, for lunch. She didn't really want to go out to a public establishment with the men. Her hands were ink-stained, and her serviceable navy suit was not what she would have chosen for luncheon in a restaurant. Beyond that, she had no desire to spend an hour forcing herself to be cordial to the contractor.

"Why not?" Her father swung around and looked at her. "Letitia, Mr. Rawley's invited us to dine with him."

She looked up and saw John Rawley's gaze resting on her. She felt a wisp of hair, escaped from her bun, tickling the back of her neck but resisted the urge to put her hand up to control it. She didn't want him to think she was preening for him. He looked her over as he would a building site, spotting the best view, weighing the assets, and noting flaws that would require changes to meet his specifications. His smile drew his lips back in an almost canine expression that sent a sick apprehension over her.

"I ought to finish the monthly books, Father," she said as placidly as she could.

"Surely you need to eat," Rawley said, smoothing each side of his blond mustache with his index finger.

The impeccable mustache had no attraction for Letitia. "Oh, I–I'll dash home for a bite, Father. Mrs. Watkins will expect us, and she'll be disappointed if neither of us comes home this noon." Letitia dipped her pen in the inkwell. "You go on." She went back to her work, hoping Rawley could not see the flush she felt creeping up from the collar of her white shirtwaist.

"All right. I'll be back in an hour," her father said, shaking his head.

Letitia thought he was a little put out with her for snubbing one of his wealthiest clients.

"Perhaps another time," Rawley said.

His silky tone almost made her shiver, and she sighed with relief as the door closed behind the two men. She estimated Rawley to be ten years her senior, and she didn't want him or anyone else in Zimmerville to think she was interested in him. Most of all, she doubted he would meet her other criteria for a potential suitor. He lacked the quiet spirit and courtesy she looked for. Above all, a man's faith mattered to her, and she doubted they would agree on that.

But her father didn't seem to consider faith as a necessary trait in a son-in-law. At least he seemed to be seriously considering Letitia's future and looking over Zimmerville's men for a suitable match. However, the three or four men her father had so far mentioned to her as worth cultivating socially were not to Letitia's taste.

Étienne had sat with his back to the room during most of the exchange, and he kept at his work in silence for another ten minutes.

The office door opened, and the broad-shouldered foreman of the lumberyard strode in, going straight to Letitia's desk. He held out a sheaf of papers, smiling.

"Mademoiselle Letitia! Here is what you need to pay my crew." He glanced toward LeClair, "*Ça va*, Étienne?"

"Ah, Jacques." Étienne looked up with a grin. "*Bien, mon ami. Et toi?* I am well, my friend, and you?"

"*Bien aussi*." To Letitia, Jacques said, "We've finished loading the flatcars with the order for Auburn. All the receipts are there for the railroad, and the slips for the men's wages."

"Thank you, Jacques." Letitia riffled through the papers and said, "That's fine. The men you hired just for this job can come in tomorrow for their pay."

"I will tell them."

Jacques Laplante had worked for Northern Lumber since he was a teenager, doing everything for the company that involved physical labor: stacking boards, cutting trees, moving logs with a team of oxen or horses, and sawing and planing lumber. He had proven himself dependable and worked his way up to lumberyard foreman.

Letitia rubbed her eyes and opened the top desk drawer, placing the records inside for future consideration.

"Mademoiselle *est fatiguée*," Jacques said.

She smiled. "Yes, I'm a little tired. How are Angelique and the children?"

They chatted for a few moments, discussing Jacques's three-month-old grandbaby, and Jacques took his leave, calling good-bye to Étienne on his way out.

The door closed, and Étienne turned slowly in his swivel chair. "Would you like to go home and eat your luncheon, Miss Hunter?" he asked. "I'll stay while you do."

"All right, thank you." Letitia always hesitated over what to call him. She wouldn't refer to him as Steve, as her father did, and she thought "Étienne" would be too intimate. . .so she avoided addressing him by name, using "Mr. LeClair" when it was absolutely necessary.

But she thought about him much more than was necessary.

To her chagrin, he seemed to think very little about her. Though forced to work more closely with her now that Weston had retired, he ignored her most of the time. He was always polite, and occasionally she caught a smile from him that kept her hope alive. Someday perhaps they could be friends. But she felt it would be improper for her to initiate such a thing, and he seemed content to keep a cool distance.

She hurried home and ate only a small portion of the food Mrs. Watkins had ready. The cook fussed about the table, complaining that she never knew whether or not anyone would come home to eat the meals she prepared.

Letitia suspected Mrs. Watkins was lonely. Of course she missed the old days, when Mother was alive. Then the house was full of people. Friends, relatives, and clients were frequent guests, and the Hunters' dinner parties were famous for the fine food, exquisite entertainment, and delightful conversation. Mrs. Watkins had headed a staff of four, and the kitchen always bustled with preparations for some event or other.

Now the big house stood empty and forlorn. Mrs. Watkins stayed on and cooked but had only Letitia and her father to cook for, and so she also had time to do a bit of cleaning. Father had discharged the two maids and the cook's helper long ago, and they relied on Mrs. Watkins and another woman who came in twice a week to do heavy cleaning.

Letitia tried to soothe the cook's injured feelings by eating a dish of pudding, though she didn't really want it. Maybe someday the house would be happy again, but she didn't see how that could happen if she and her father spent all their energy on the lumber company.

She headed back to the office, wondering if her father had yet returned. Being alone in the office with Étienne was becoming awkward. Not that he did anything to make her feel that way—quite the opposite. She mentally ticked off his attributes as she hurried along the sidewalk. He was prompt, courteous, neat, efficient, respectful of her father, and diligent at his work. She told herself she didn't consider his looks. To her, the mental and spiritual aspects of a man took precedence over the physical.

If she could bring herself to acknowledge it, though, she would also have admitted that he was quite handsome. He was strong; she'd had ample proof of that when he carried her from the pond to the bunkhouse at Spruce Run and again when he'd cleared a path for the sleigh. His features were well defined and pleasant to look at. In fact, it was disconcerting having a man so good-looking in the office. She'd resolved from the outset not to embarrass him or herself—or her father, for that matter—by ogling him. She'd cultivated a cool but courteous manner and downcast eyes. No one else seemed to have an inkling that her heart raced whenever she thought about him. It helped that he sat with his back to the room when working. For eight hours a day she mostly saw his broad shoulders. There were worse things to look at.

She hurried along, admonishing herself to stop letting her thoughts stray into an unprofitable avenue. Even if Étienne should ever notice her the way she noticed him, her father would never consider the Canadian an acceptable suitor for his only daughter.

When she stepped into the office, Étienne turned in his chair, and she smiled at him.

"You go ahead for your lunch now, Mr. LeClair."

"Thank you, but I brought a lunch my landlady packed for me, and I ate it while you were gone. Your father will not mind that, will he?"

"Oh, no, I don't think so, as long as there were no customers in here at the time. But you are entitled to go out for a while if you wish."

He sat watching her as she returned to her desk.

"The order for the courthouse is quite complex," he said

tentatively, and Letitia snapped her eyes up to his. Was he making an overture of sorts?

"Yes," she agreed. "It will take several months to bring in everything Mr. Rawley wants, I think."

LeClair nodded, his gaze not leaving her face.

It was unnerving for Letitia. During the workday, she often found herself gazing at the nape of his neck, where the dark hair was trimmed abruptly above his collar. Having the tables turned, with him appraising her, caused a slip in her usual calm demeanor. She dropped her gaze and reached for her pen.

"I suppose he will come here often to see about the lumber?" Étienne asked.

"I hope not." She realized she had spoken out of turn and added quickly, "We will deliver it to his building site as soon as we have each load ready."

Étienne nodded, his face grave. "And Mr. Hunter, he feels better now?"

"Yes, I think so. Thank you for asking."

"His color is better since we came back here."

She nodded. "I believe the journey strained him. But he's back to his own home and the cook who knows his digestive habits well. He seems fine now."

"That is good." He stood up. "I will be back soon."

She watched him walk to the door. He was tall, and his black suit jacket, although cut from inexpensive material, hung from his shoulders with a flair. With money for the right clothes, he could be a striking figure. When the door closed behind him, she jerked her attention back to her task. *You are a foolish girl*, she remonstrated. *You have no call to think of this man in that manner.*

She took out the men's pay slips and added them, then wrote the amount on a slip for the bank. *Or any man, for that matter.*

She laid the pen down and rested her head in her hands with her elbows on the desk. She had let herself imagine something between herself and Étienne. She was lonely; she recognized that. But he must be lonely, too. Would it be wrong for a friendship to develop between them? And if it did, would she be content to keep it at that? He had begun the fragmented conversation today, while her father was out. Was it significant? Or was he merely attempting to put her at ease? Had he sensed her embarrassment when Rawley spoke to her? Or was she imagining his interest?

Did he have a sweetheart back in Quebec? Was that the reason he'd been so distant toward her all month? Had he come here to save enough money to make his marriage feasible?

Dear Lord, she prayed silently, *help me not to engage in foolish speculations. You know what is best for me. I feel such a longing for friendship with Étienne, but I don't wish to displease my father. Please take this desire away from me if it's wrong. And I do ask that You would meet Étienne's needs, whatever they are. He's so far from his family. I know he's found a church home here. He has kept a distance between us, both inside this office and out, as I have. I think that is best. I don't want to cause him any distress, and I want to please You.*

☙

Étienne leaned against the end of a stack of lumber where René Ouellette sat, eating the lunch Sophie had packed for him in a lard pail. He would have joined René in sitting on the boards, but he didn't want to get sawdust all over his suit. The March sun held some warmth, bringing out the sharp smell of newly cut lumber and melting the little snow that lurked in the corners of the lumberyard.

He didn't always take a break outside the office at noon. Most days Mr. Hunter and Letitia went home for lunch, and he ate at his desk and reopened the office afterward. But today Letitia had returned before her father, and he'd felt just a bit of awkwardness in the situation.

She had not rebuffed him when he spoke to her, but neither had she seemed eager to continue the conversation, so he had decided to get some fresh air and give her a few minutes alone.

From his post near the lumber pile, he could see almost to the door of the office and knew he could tell if her father returned or a customer arrived.

"You are getting on well in the office," René said.

Étienne nodded. "It goes fine most days. Today. . ."

"What happened?"

Étienne hesitated, realizing he did not want to discuss the feelings nagging at the back of his mind. He spread his hands and shrugged. "It is nothing. Just a client, one of the contractors who does business with Monsieur Hunter. He is a man full of himself."

"A rich man?"

"I would say so."

"What is it about him that bothers you? Does he treat you poorly?"

"Not really." Étienne thought back to John Rawley's manner when they discussed his order. "No, he did not seem prejudiced against me."

"That is good," René said. "Sometimes men like that treat us bad. They think we are stupid, and they yell at us and blame us for things that are not our fault."

Étienne nodded as he thought about that. "He was not that way."

"What about the boss?"

"No, he treats me well."

René shuddered. "I don't see how you can be in the same room with him all the time. Me, I would have a nervous condition if he stood over me while I worked."

Étienne smiled at that. "It's not like that. He lets me alone most of the time, and I write my letters and keep the records. And now I suppose I'd better get back at it."

He left René and strolled toward the office. It was not Lincoln Hunter who'd tested his nerves today. It was Rawley, but not in his manner toward Étienne. He didn't seem to care that the clerk was a Frenchman, only that he knew where to get the materials he wanted and could offer the best prices.

No, it was his attitude toward Miss Hunter. Rawley hadn't said much, but the way he'd looked at Letitia had heated Étienne's blood. One quick glance was enough; then he'd forced himself to keep his eyes on his ledger.

But he'd seen Rawley's smug, predatory appraisal of Letitia. Immediately, a protective rage had risen in Étienne's heart. But her father said nothing. Nothing!

No, that wasn't true. Her father had actually tried to coax her into going along to have lunch with the man, while Letitia was clearly uncomfortable at the suggestion.

If I could speak up, he thought as he neared the office. *If I had the right. . .*

But that train of thought was useless. He would never have that right. If he were on an equal social footing with such a lovely woman, he would never pursue her with the arrogance Rawley had exhibited. And if it were within his power, he would not expose her to such a crass man. Was her father blind? Could he not see the possessive way Rawley had looked his daughter over? Or did he simply not care?

Maybe the boss wanted to marry Letitia off to a rich man.

Étienne shook his head. If that were the case, putting her in an office day in and day out and dressing her in the plain garb of a workingwoman was not the way to entice the prey. Letitia should be at home in the fine mansion on High Street, pampered and coddled, swathed in silks and velvets, and Mr. Hunter ought to have parties and balls where the tycoons could meet her in a social setting.

Instead, her father treated her like a servant.

Last week Étienne had gone to the bank alone for the first time, to get the payroll money on Friday. Letitia had prepared the bank order, totaling the amounts on her worksheet while he watched. To his surprise, her name was not among those receiving a paycheck. Her father's draw was there, and all the names of the employees, including his own, from the sawmill and lumberyard foremen down to the boy who shoveled shavings from under the planer. But not Letitia Hunter's.

He concluded that Letitia served unpaid. She might see it as her contribution to the family. Étienne saw it as something else: stinginess on her father's part and a lack of true paternal love. She was a precious gem, and her father ought to guard her!

As he reached the office door, he saw Mr. Hunter half a block down the street, returning from his lunch with Rawley. Étienne determined to put the incident from his mind. Thinking about it would only embitter him toward the boss and perhaps cause him to say something he would regret.

He pushed open the door and stepped inside. As his eyes adjusted to the dim interior, he saw that Letitia was looking up at him.

She smiled. "Welcome back." This time she did not look away.

He returned her smile, and the errant thought whispered in his mind once more, *If I had the right...*

For a moment they held the pose, looking into each other's eyes across the room. There was so much he wished he could change, so much he wanted to say.

A step behind him prompted him to break the gaze and turn in the doorway.

"Good afternoon, Mr. Hunter. Let me take your hat and coat, sir."

seven

"I'll be over at Mark Warren's office for the next hour or so. I need to have him go over this contract with me." Lincoln Hunter stopped by Étienne's desk. "Steve, I expect Tappy Pinkham to come in and pay his last installment today. You handle it if he comes while I'm gone." The boss breezed out the door, letting in a blast of April wind.

Étienne felt anticipation as he dipped his steel pen in the inkwell. The times when Mr. Hunter left the office during the day were a sweet torture for him.

Since John Rawley had placed his order a month ago, something had changed between him and Letitia. She greeted Étienne with a lilt in her voice each morning, and he found it more and more difficult to keep his eyes off her.

He was glad old Weston had chosen to face his desk toward the window. It was growing harder to conceal his elation when he found his lovely coworker's gaze—dare he think of it as *tender*—on him. Her smiles, more frequent now, were treasures he tucked away in his memory to be recounted and cherished later.

This wonderful distraction alternated between thrilling him and distressing him. After all, nothing could come of the feelings growing so lush in his heart. Was it wrong to let the small gestures of friendship flourish between them? He didn't think he could stop, now that he'd begun to go beyond courtesy and show her a glimpse of the esteem he felt for her.

Sundays were even worse, when he saw her at church, usually in the pew with the Laplante family. He'd taken to sitting a couple of rows behind them, where he could see the back of Letitia's head. She always sat so demurely, the picture of attentive devotion. Sometimes she turned her head a bit to share her hymnal with one of the children, and he saw her profile. That image always sent a tremor of longing through him. Night after night, his prayers ended with, "And Father, if You could send me a woman so faithful and sweet to be my wife. . ."

He couldn't specifically ask that God would give him Letitia. Could he? No, that was unthinkable. Knowing he thought the unthinkable brought on waves of guilt.

Even before Mr. Hunter's footsteps died away as he left for the meeting with his attorney, Étienne struggled with these thoughts, and he looked out the window in an attempt to clear his mind.

"Mr. LeClair?"

He inhaled carefully, savoring his name on her lips. Dared he ask her to call him by his first name?

"Yes, mademoiselle?" He turned and met her gaze.

Her cheeks bore a charming flush. "I am finished with these orders. Do you need to see them again?"

"Oh, I am done with those, thank you."

"Then I shall file them away." Her blue eyes met his for a long instant, and his pulse caught and then rushed on.

She rose and went to the cabinet across the room where old documents were kept. He knew it would be impolite to stare at her as she worked, so he turned back toward his desk. He'd discovered that when the light was right, he could see her reflection in the window, and he couldn't resist catching a glimpse. Even in her plain blue skirt and white blouse, she was lovely. In his heart, she was as beautiful as any princess.

As she opened the cupboard door, he remembered the day he had lifted her slender form, so heavy and cold, and carried her from the pond to the bunkhouse at Spruce Run. The knowledge that he would never again have the chance to hold her in his arms saddened him. Why were his affections fastened on this unattainable woman? Why hadn't God led him to a young Canadian woman of his own class?

The office door opened abruptly, and a tall man came in, slamming the door behind him against the wind. He pulled off his hat, exposing his blond hair, and Étienne recognized Rawley, the contractor who was building the new courthouse.

Rawley glanced at him, then turned the other direction. His gaze swept over Lincoln Hunter's vacant desk and chair, then landed on Letitia.

"Ah, Miss Hunter. Your father is not in?"

Letitia closed the cabinet door. "No, he has gone out for a while. Is there anything Mr. LeClair can help you with?"

Étienne stood quickly, but Rawley only gave him a quick glance and took a step closer to Letitia.

"No, I don't think so. But if you don't mind, I'd like to leave a message with you for Mr. Hunter."

"Of course."

Letitia's features went wooden, and she walked briskly to her desk. "Would you like to write him a note?"

Rawley followed her and leaned across the desk as she sat down behind it. "No, that's all right. It's only that he told me a week or so ago that he expected the shipment from Boston soon."

Letitia looked past him, and Étienne caught a flicker of dismay in her face as her gaze connected with his. Was Rawley's stance and his nearness to her making her uncomfortable?

Étienne hesitated no longer but strode toward Rawley.

"Perhaps I can assist you, sir. That shipment has not yet arrived, but it is true we look for it any day. We can send a boy around to tell you when it comes in."

Rawley straightened and rounded slowly to face him. Étienne received the distinct impression that the contractor was not pleased with his interference.

"Yes. That would be most helpful. Thank you, LeClair." Rawley turned his back on Étienne. "Well, Miss Hunter, now that that is settled, there is something else I'd like to discuss with you."

Étienne stood still for a moment, uncertain of how to react. The contractor had dismissed him, no question. Should he fade into the woodwork and resume his post at his desk? One more look at Letitia's tense face rooted Étienne to the spot.

"And what would that be, Mr. Rawley?" She avoided looking up at him, but pulled a sheet of paper to her and began scribbling on it with a pencil.

Rawley gave Étienne a pointed look, and he gulped and stepped back, closer to his own desk.

What should I do, heavenly Father? Étienne sat down slowly. He was certain Rawley hoped he would leave the office, but it would take a locomotive to get him out of here when Letitia clearly didn't want to be left alone with the customer.

"Well, I was hoping you'd do me a favor."

"I?" Letitia's voice rose in doubt.

"Why, yes. Last month I invited you to join your father and me for luncheon, but you said it was inconvenient. I've done a lot of thinking about that, and I can see that it was shortsighted of me. Of course you wouldn't want to go out in the middle of the day in your working attire. So I thought perhaps you would make up my disappointment to me."

"Really, sir, there is no reason to feel badly."

Étienne sneaked a glance. Letitia's face was reddening, and she shook her head in protest.

"Oh, but there is. You can allow me to undo my gaffe by agreeing to have dinner with me one evening."

Étienne sat very still, holding his breath and waiting for Letitia's answer.

"Thank you, but I don't think—"

"Please?" Rawley's voice took on a soft wheedle. "It would give you a chance to dress up. You must not get out much. I never see you in any of the restaurants. I'd love to show you the new dining room at the Highland Hotel."

"Thank you, Mr. Rawley, but—"

"Wonderful!" he cried.

"No!" Her consternation caused Étienne to wince, and he had to force himself to stay in his chair and not look her way.

"No?" Rawley asked. "You don't mean that."

"I do. Mr. Rawley, I don't wish to go with you." Her voice was firmer now.

"But it will be a diversion for you. A pleasant evening."

"I said no."

"Look, Letitia, if you're worried about what your father will say, I assure you—"

Étienne sprang to his feet. "Excuse me, Mr. Rawley, but I think you should leave now."

Letitia's gaze met his with such relief that he stepped toward the contractor with confidence.

Rawley squared his shoulders and turned slowly toward him. "I beg your pardon?"

Étienne cleared his throat. "I think that the lady would prefer that you leave."

Rawley's face was flushed, and his eyes narrowed. "And I think that you've overstepped your place."

There was a moment's silence as they took each other's measure; then Letitia's gentle voice sliced the crackling air.

"I meant what I said, Mr. Rawley. I don't wish to go out, but I thank you for the invitation. Now, I've written down your message for my father, and I will let him know you inquired about the Boston shipment."

Rawley's lower jaw flexed; then he glanced at her and back toward Étienne.

"Fine." He strode out the door and banged it shut.

Étienne breathed a prayer of thanks and turned to look at Letitia. She was sitting very still, her eyes closed and her cheeks nearly as pale as they were when he fished her from the pond.

"Mademoiselle," he said, "I hope I did not add to your discomfort."

"No." She opened her eyes and gave him a chagrinned smile. "Not at all. Thank you."

He nodded, satisfied. No matter what future revenge Rawley devised against him, it was worth it.

"Could I get you some tea?" he asked.

Her eyes widened in surprise. "That's not necessary."

"No, but it might do us both some good."

A genuine smile lit her face. "Perhaps you are right. Thank you."

He went to the woodstove between her desk and her father's and took the teapot and a cup down from the shelf above. It took only a minute to measure tea from the tin and pour the water from the kettle they kept simmering.

When he placed her cup carefully on her desk, she again looked up at him with those startling blue eyes. "Won't you join me?"

"I. . .well, yes, thank you." He poured himself a cupful and took it back to his desk. Could he move his chair closer to hers? That might be presumptuous. He turned it to face her and sat down two yards from her desk.

Letitia lifted her cup to her lips. Étienne did the same. He hadn't let it steep long enough, and it was weak, but she didn't seem to care as she continued to sip the hot brew.

He smiled at her. "You are feeling better, is it not so?"

"Yes, I am. I cannot thank you enough, Mr.—Mr. LeClair."

"Please. Étienne."

She nodded, her face set in grave, almost sorrowful, lines. Should he have told her to call him Steve, as her father did? No, if they were to be friends, as he truly believed she wished to be, then she would not mind calling him by his own name.

"I—would you—?" She pressed her lips together and stared down into her teacup, then met his gaze once more and said, a little breathless, "Do you think you could call me Letitia?"

He hesitated.

"Oh, not when Father is here."

Her hasty disclaimer had him holding back a smile. This was the way it had to be, but it was a step forward. He nodded. "It would be an honor."

They sat in silence for several seconds, and slowly her lips quivered upward. Étienne inhaled deeply. In the deep recesses of his mind, it seemed there was something he ought to be doing this morning, but he couldn't for the life of him recall what it was. It couldn't be as important as watching Letitia, seeing her relax moment by moment. She lost the worried air and settled back in her chair, cradling her warm cup in her hands and looking at him.

Someone knocked, and the door opened. A farmer bundled in a wool coat and knit hat entered. Étienne set his cup on his desk and jumped up, turning his chair around quickly.

"May I help you, sir?"

"I've come to pay my bill. Pinkham's the name."

"Certainly. I have your account right here, sir." He reached for the sheet of paper on his desk.

The man settled the bill and took his leave. Étienne closed the door behind him and handed Letitia the money.

"I had better write up the invoices now," he told her with an apologetic smile.

"Yes, I have some details to attend to as well."

As he resumed his usual post at the desk, a warm contentment settled on him.

The door swung open once more, and Mr. Hunter stomped in. "Letitia, I just saw John Rawley down the street."

Étienne kept his head down and wrote the date on the sheet of paper he would use for the first invoice.

"He came here looking for you about half an hour ago," Letitia said. "I told him we would notify him when his shipment comes in."

Étienne marveled at her serene tone.

"Really, Letitia! I don't know why you continue to reject that man's advances. He's from a good family, and he has a thriving business."

"Please, Father. Could we discuss this later, in private?" Her voice was strained now, and Étienne wished that this time he had an excuse to leave the room.

"I see no reason why you can't give him a little encouragement."

"He is a client, Father. I try to keep a professional relationship with all your clients."

The boss uttered a sound somewhere between a snort and a grunt. "You need to understand, Letitia, that John Rawley is one of my biggest customers. I rely on men like him for a living. He can be difficult at times, it's true, but business with him might go more smoothly if you were to show him a sweeter disposition."

Étienne froze in his chair. His stomach churned. How could Hunter address his daughter in that manner? Was he suggesting it was part of her job to beguile the customers?

After a moment of silence, Letitia choked out, "Please, Father. I cannot abide the man."

"Oh, and why not, may I ask? He's perfectly courteous."

"I do not find him so. And if you must know, when I went to the bank last week, I saw him coming out of that. . . establishment across the way."

"What, the Loon? He probably had lunch there."

"It's a tavern, Father."

"Most taverns serve good, plain food."

"He was—" Letitia stopped, then whispered, "He was with another man, and he was rather boisterous. And I don't wish to discuss it further."

A long silence was followed by the creak of the boss's chair at the far end of the room and the slamming of a desk drawer.

Étienne realized he'd copied the figures for the invoice without thinking about them. He laid down his pen and went over the sheet to be sure he'd written everything correctly. The quiet in the office was painful. Perhaps he should have stayed in the woods.

eight

The following Monday afternoon, a merchant came in to discuss with Lincoln Hunter the materials needed for the construction of a new store, and Letitia and Étienne were left to deal with several men who came in to pay their bills as the end of the month approached.

Letitia had hoped to get away after lunch and do some shopping at the Harris Emporium. Her shirtwaists were becoming stained and frayed at the cuffs, and she hadn't had a new dress in two years. She knew she could count on Mrs. Harris, the lovely widow who ran the women's clothing shop, to help her pick out suitable wear for the office and a nicer dress for church.

Sometimes Letitia envied Mrs. Harris. She had run the business herself since her husband died two years earlier. The eligible men of Zimmerville watched her with uneasy admiration. The women loved to shop in her establishment, as she had an unerring sense of fashion tempered by practicality, but they gossiped about her independence. Mrs. Harris seemed to enjoy her self-reliance and was not yet ready to have a man take care of her again.

But today was not the day to visit the emporium. The customers continued to come and go, and several employees came in on errands from the lumberyard and sawmill.

At 2:30 an errand boy from the railroad depot dashed in. Seeing that Mr. Hunter was busy, he went to Letitia's desk and handed her a slip of paper. She was used to receiving this sort of communication from the stationmaster, and gave the boy a nickel and sent him on his way.

After deciphering the note, she went to stand near her

father's desk, waiting for a break in his conversation.

"Yes, we can get you clear pine for that," he told his client. "It may take a few days to collect as much as you want in that quality." He glanced up at Letitia. "What is it?"

"Excuse me," she said. "Mr. Kreedle sent a note saying the large order for Mr. Rawley is at the station. He thinks it will be three wagonloads, at least."

"Fine; tell Laplante." As she turned away to carry out her father's request, he called after her, "Oh, and go round and tell Mr. Rawley, too. He'll want to be ready when our men get there to unload."

Letitia turned to see if he truly intended for her to take the message personally, but he was already listening to a story the customer was telling.

She hovered for a moment in the middle of the room, then went to the coat tree. Perhaps Jacques Laplante would assign one of his men to do the unpleasant chore for her. She reached for her shawl and spread it over her hair, tucking the ends together at her throat, then took her coat from its hook.

"Pardon me," Étienne said softly behind her.

She whirled, surprised to find him so close.

"I couldn't help but hear." He glanced toward her father. "Forgive me if I presume too much, but you might be more at ease if I were the one to carry this message to Rawley's place of business."

"Why. . .thank you. I was hoping one of Jacques's men could go."

"He will need them all at the depot."

She nodded, knowing it was true, and bit her bottom lip. "Do you mind?"

"No. At least, not so much as I would mind sitting here trying to work while I wondered what became of you on this errand."

She looked down at the bare oak floor. She could read his unspoken thoughts—her father ought not to have told her to go to Rawley's office alone. It was unacceptable, at least in the perception of a gentleman like Étienne.

"He doesn't mean to be thoughtless," she whispered.

Étienne's gaze darted past her toward the other men, and he said softly. "*Tout* est bien. . .all is well. And I shall tell Jacques first, so you need not worry about that, either."

He grabbed his hat and jacket and hurried out the door. Letitia went back to her desk with some relief. However, her father's dark scowl did nothing to reassure her.

Ten minutes later, Étienne had not returned when her father saw the customer out the door. He turned around, his eyebrows lowered, the lines at the corners of his mouth deeper than normal, and fixed his gaze on Letitia.

"Why are you letting LeClair do favors for you?"

She stared up at him in surprise. "He offered to go."

"Oh, yes, he offered. I asked you to take that message. LeClair has plenty of work to do."

"Father, please." She felt the mild pain that preceded tears forming in her eyes. "You know I dislike Mr. Rawley. It baffles me why you would purposely put me in his path. You would never have asked Mother to do something like that."

Her father stood still for a moment, glaring at her, and Letitia wanted to run. Her father had disappointed her many times, but he had never frightened her before.

At last he sighed and pulled Étienne's chair out. Sagging into it, he ran his hand through his silvery hair. "All right. I give up. You don't like him."

"I don't."

Her father nodded and exhaled heavily. "I don't know what to do with you, Letitia."

"You don't?" She smiled and shook her head. "I'd say you do. You put me behind a desk, and here I've been for more than two years."

"Do you hate it?"

"No. But. . ."

"But what, child?"

She looked about the room, unsure how to begin, or even whether or not she wanted to. At last she brought her sights back to him. "I don't wish to work in this office all my life."

"So you've told me before."

"I. . .haven't meant to complain, Father."

"I don't say you have. No, what you're telling me is reasonable. It's been easy to let things go on as they have, but—" He sighed and sat back a little, eyeing her at length. "You are quite grown up, daughter."

"Yes, I am, Father. I shall be one and twenty in the fall."

"I thought perhaps you might see something commendable in a man like John Rawley."

She picked up her pen and the rag she used to wipe it with. "Must I marry one of your clients?"

"I wouldn't say you have to. It might further my interests. But, no, you don't have to."

"Thank you," she whispered.

"I suppose we ought to entertain more and give you a chance to meet prospective suitors in a more congenial setting than this." His gesture encompassed the stark office.

"You needn't do that."

"Oh? And where do you expect to find a husband, if not here?" His eyes flared suddenly and he stood up. "Don't even think it, Letitia!"

She felt the blood rush to her cheeks. "What?"

Her father walked to her desk and leaned down, gripping its edge. "LeClair is a common laborer who grew up in a hovel in some hamlet in Quebec. I plucked him out of a lumber camp." His voice grew louder, and his eyes flashed. "Do you think I would ever consent—?"

She shoved back her chair and stood facing him, her knees trembling. "He is a fine man and a good clerk. I've heard you say so."

"What, and you think I'd marry my daughter off to a clerk?

You know what the man earns."

"I don't know where you've gotten this notion, Father. Mr. LeClair offered to carry out a distasteful errand for me. There has been nothing between us. Why you think he would aspire to winning my hand, I've no idea. He is a gentleman; that is all. And he is an excellent clerk."

Her father's lips pursed and the fire in his eyes died down. "He's been quick to learn his new duties; I'll give him that."

"I heard you tell Mark Warren he's invaluable to you."

"He has potential."

"You ought to pay him accordingly."

"Ha! Watch your tongue, girl! You're awfully concerned about this clerk in whom you have no interest."

Letitia sat down and covered her face with her hands, taking slow, deep breaths. *Lord, forgive me,* she cried silently. *How could I be so defiant? Father is right.*

She looked up, and he still towered over the desk, scowling down at her.

"I'm sorry."

"Hmph."

Her tears flowed freely then. "Forgive me, Father. I should not have spoken to you in that manner."

He straightened and did not meet her eyes. "Well, there now. No need to get all riled up, is there?"

She shook her head and opened her desk drawer in search of a handkerchief.

"We'll say no more about it, then. You know how I feel."

"Yes, Father." *But you don't know how I feel,* her heart cried.

"I'd say it's time we had a social event at the house."

She stared at him, unable to respond.

"Several clients have contracted large orders with us recently, and I always used to entertain them in celebration of such events."

"Are you thinking. . .a dinner party?"

"Yes. Can you arrange it with Mrs. Watkins?"

Letitia gulped. "I'll speak to her this evening. How many people?"

"Well, let's see. There's Eldon Bane and his wife, and Clive Wheaton. I assume he's married. George Young might come, but he lives over in Shawmut. And there's Rawley, and Mark Warren and his wife. How many is that?"

Letitia did a quick tally. "Ten, I think, if they all come. Mr. Young is a widower, is he not?"

"Yes, and you'd do well to buy a new dress for the occasion."

She lowered her pencil and eyed him suspiciously. "What does my wardrobe have to do with Mr. Young?"

He held up his hands in defense. "I shan't push you, but you want to make a good match, don't you?"

"And Mr. Young is your idea of a good one?"

Her father shrugged. "He's a bit older than you, but—"

"A bit? Father, he's your age!"

"Nonsense. He can't be over forty."

"That's much too old for me."

He frowned and strode toward his desk. "All right, but the least you can do is look for a husband whose business will complement mine."

"Father! I thought the subject was closed."

He frowned at her. "I shan't force you into a marriage you don't want. But you've told me you want to marry."

"I do, someday. But not just any man, Father."

"Fine. I give you leave to refuse any man who doesn't suit you. But, Letitia, if you must marry and leave me in the lurch here, lacking a clerk, you can at least look for a man with a good business head on his shoulders. And be prepared to play the gracious hostess at that dinner party!"

"Yes, Father."

She wanted to ask him if he must include John Rawley in the guest list, but their argument had left her drained, and she didn't want to take a chance on starting another.

A new customer came through the door, and she lowered

her head over the papers on her desk. As she had hoped, her father greeted the man and drew him to the far end of the room. She closed her eyes for a moment. *Lord, please forgive my anger and my behavior toward my father. And please, Lord, I don't feel confident that Father will find the right man for me. I'm going to leave that up to You. It's clear I can't consider ever forming an attachment for Étienne. I must forget that.*

An ache in her chest told her that it was too late. She'd known it was impossible, and yet she had allowed the hope to grow. And after today, she was fairly certain Étienne harbored feelings for her, too. But that could never come to fruition. She would have to let him know somehow that they could never allow their friendship to blossom into anything more. Would that hurt him as much as it was hurting her? In addition to the pain of separation, she was hit with a monstrous guilt.

She had allowed his hope to spring up, too. And now she had to kill it.

nine

Letitia raised her arms and let the maid ease her new gown of orchid silk chiffon over her head. It floated down around her in a soft cloud, and she couldn't resist swirling a bit and watching the skirt billow.

The maid smiled at her. "Shall I do your buttons now, miss?"

Agnes, Mrs. Watkins's niece, had agreed to aid her aunt in preparing for the dinner party and help Letitia get dressed. Letitia had also engaged their biweekly cleaning woman to put in extra time scrubbing the house and polishing everything in sight. Her father had assured her a few days earlier that he had employed a man to act as their butler that night.

The dinner party was the most exciting event at the Hunter home in years, and Letitia couldn't deny her anticipation. Even if the guest list was not of her own choosing, she was sure she could find someone to converse with. *Even the customers' wives must have something to talk about,* she thought as Agnes fastened the buttons on the back of her dress.

Agnes turned her around and stroked a wisp of Letitia's hair into place. "You look beautiful, miss."

"Thank you." Letitia smiled and sent the girl down the back stairs to the kitchen to help with the last-minute chaos there. She picked up her gloves and fan, then paused for one last look in the mirror.

She hadn't been looking at herself much lately. On work mornings, she donned serviceable clothing for the office and took a cursory glance in the glass to be sure she looked neat and efficient.

Now she caught her breath. The gown was the perfect color, a brighter shade than she'd first chosen. But Mrs. Harris, the

owner of the emporium, had assured her the orchid was more
flattering than the pale lavender, and that it was all the fashion
in Boston this year.

"You don't want to look dowdy," she'd said, smiling at Letitia
and cocking her head to one side.

"Well, no," Letitia had replied. "But I don't wish to be. . .
daring, either."

Mrs. Harris laughed, showing her even, white teeth. "No
worries there, my dear. The design you've chosen is far from
audacious. In fact, I was thinking perhaps we could alter the
neckline just a bit—"

"No!" Letitia had winced at her own sharpness. "I'm sorry.
I. . .wish to be modest, even for an evening party."

Mrs. Harris nodded, smiling. "I see that. Simplicity is
definitely the look for you. But you can be both modest and
fashionable. What would you say to some of this elegant
Duchesse lace for the collar?"

Now Letitia could see the wisdom in the widow's sug-
gestions. The lines of the gown Mrs. Harris and the dress-
maker she employed had sewn for her set off Letitia's figure
and creamy complexion. Her blue eyes seemed darker than
usual against the vivid orchid backdrop, and Letitia was
pleased with the upswept hairdo she and Agnes had managed
together. Of course, the man she cared about would not be
there to see her tonight. She must put all thoughts of Étienne
out of her mind and be open to the Lord's leading.

Well, at least I shan't be embarrassed about my clothes, she
thought. A prayer formed in her heart, and she sent it winging
heavenward. *Lord, let me please Father tonight, if possible, and let
our guests be glad that they came.*

She inhaled deeply and left her room for the main stairway.
The thud of the knocker resounded through the house. Below
her in the hall, a man in a black suit was heading toward
the front door. The temporary butler, Letitia surmised. She
slipped quickly down the steps and into the parlor, where her

father and several guests stood before the fireplace with glasses in their hands.

"Ah, Letitia," her father said. His gaze swept over her, and he seemed a bit relieved, bestowing on her a smile of approval. "You've met my daughter?" he asked, turning toward his guests.

"Oh, my," said a large, florid man, staring at her in wonder. "This isn't the little lady I've seen at the office?"

Letitia felt her cheeks redden, but smiled and extended her hand. "Why, yes, Mr. Young. We've met several times."

"Oh, but you weren't got up like this, my dear. Why, your father shouldn't hide you away like that! Once you're seen in that gown, you'll be invited to social events all over the county."

She knew her face was scarlet now but was at a loss for words. *This is the man Father hinted was interested in courting me? Oh, no, please, Lord!* The man was as old as she'd guessed, if not older, and his nose was uncommonly large. She allowed him to grasp her hand while she sought a suitable response.

To her relief, her father said, "And you know Mr. and Mrs. Warren."

Letitia nodded and extricated her hand from Mr. Young's, then extended it to the attorney's wife. "Welcome, Mrs. Warren. Thank you for coming."

"You look splendid, my dear," Mrs. Warren said. "That color suits you."

Lincoln Hunter looked toward the doorway and cried, "Clive! So glad you could make it. And Mrs. Wheaton, I don't believe you've met my daughter, Letitia."

The Banes, who were owners of a feed and grain business, arrived next. Letitia smiled until her face ached and drew the wives away from the men, inquiring about children and grandchildren. She was soon at ease and realized the three other women were carrying at least their share of the conversation, talking about gardening, dressmaking, and the difficulty of finding household help.

John Rawley was the last to arrive, and Letitia turned away as he entered, quickly asking Mrs. Wheaton a question so that she need not meet his imperious gaze. She heard her father and the other men greet him heartily and welcome Rawley into their circle.

Her father put a glass in Rawley's hand, and he lifted it to his lips. Letitia had to hide her smile behind her fan when she saw the change in his expression. Her father had assured her that he would adhere to the family's tradition, faithfully followed when her mother was alive, of not serving alcohol in the house. Only the magnitude of her relief revealed to her how much she had feared he would change that custom. Rawley, however, seemed unpleasantly surprised.

Mr. Young soon worked his way to a spot at Letitia's elbow, and she was forced to include him in the chatter. After that, the small knots of people broke and reformed several times.

Rawley's greeting when he approached her was more subdued than usual, and Letitia wondered if he still smarted from her refusal to go out to dinner with him.

"That's a lovely gown," he murmured in her ear when the other guests were distracted.

"Thank you." Letitia took a step away from him, but he followed.

"I knew you must have something nicer than those plain duds you wear in the office."

She glared at him. "Really, sir!"

He chuckled and opened his mouth again, but at that moment Mark Warren claimed his attention, and Letitia escaped to join Mrs. Bane and Mrs. Warren, who were discussing a mission project both were involved in at the large church downtown.

Letitia felt a moment of panic. That was the church her family used to attend. What if someone asked her why she hadn't been there for the past year? This wasn't how she wanted her father to learn of her choice. Though Lincoln Hunter himself did not care to attend any longer, she felt sure he'd disapprove of his daughter leaving the big church and joining a smaller, less formal congregation.

A moment later an expectant hush fell over the company, and Letitia glanced toward the doorway. The temporary butler stood in the arch, his face impassive. As all the guests turned toward him, he looked toward Letitia's father and received an almost imperceptible nod from him.

It couldn't be.

It was.

A mixture of dismay, wonder, and rage crashed over Letitia.

"Dinner is served," said Étienne.

❧

Étienne tried to keep his gaze from straying to Letitia. It was one of the hardest things he had ever done.

The rich purple silk dress she wore seemed plain at first glance, but he realized almost at once that it was not. Understated, perhaps, but the lines and flow of the shimmering fabric were anything but common.

But it was not the special dress that tempted his eyes so sorely. It was Letitia's face, and the stricken look that clouded her beautiful features when she recognized him.

Étienne watched Mr. Hunter offer his arm to one of the visiting ladies, and he knew it was time for him to go to the dining room. He took a deep breath and turned, not meeting Letitia's eyes. He couldn't bear to see the distress there.

It was crucial that he stay calm through the rest of the evening, but his heart pounded and his stomach churned. He had made a mistake. Seeing him tonight had upset her, and he would gladly have forgone the extra money he was earning to avoid hurting her.

He stood straight and still by the kitchen door, where Mrs. Watkins, the cook, had told him to, waiting for the guests to enter. Outwardly he must appear steady and emotionless, but his mind was in upheaval. Somehow, without meaning to, he had brought pain to the woman he loved.

That admission sent his pulse racing even faster. It was true, although he could never admit it to anyone or declare it to Letitia. He loved her! He watched the doorway, eager for another glimpse of her.

She entered on Mr. Young's arm. Étienne had waited on the man twice at the office. Young owned a farm south of town and had come to Northern Lumber to select materials for a large new barn. The big man could scarcely take his eyes off Letitia, and Étienne couldn't blame him. Letitia's appearance tonight was perfection, and Étienne knew that she was lovely within, too. He forced back a twinge of jealousy. He had no right to object. The widower pulled out her chair, smiling at her and saying something he no doubt thought witty. Letitia, the charming hostess, smiled back, but without a trace of coquetry. Étienne wondered if she was enjoying the party or enduring it the best she could, to please her father. Her demeanor suggested something in between, and he was relieved. Her guests could not fault her in her genuine hospitality.

Letitia sat at one end of the table, opposite her father. On either side of her were Young and Rawley. Étienne waited until they were all seated, then opened the kitchen door a crack and signaled to the cook that it was time. Mrs. Watkins carried a large, covered china dish to him. The soup tureen, she had told him earlier. It was a new word in his English vocabulary, but he grasped the handles firmly.

"Be careful now," she whispered. "Don't be spilling my onion soup on the floor in front of company."

Étienne nodded and carried the heavy dish into the dining room.

The guests looked his way in anticipation, and he walked cautiously. He mustn't stumble tonight. In most situations, the stares of the people would not bother him. They were only interested in their dinner, not in the man who carried it. But once again, Étienne saw Letitia glance his way, then quickly avert her eyes.

He should have mentioned his intention to her yesterday at the office, but there had been no chance when her father wasn't present. No, he shouldn't have agreed to this arrangement without her knowledge. He felt a flush rise from beneath his stiff collar and flood his face, but not for himself. His embarrassment was for Letitia.

⋙

Letitia smiled and answered her guests' comments and sipped her water. She even permitted Étienne to serve her a bowl of soup. All the time, her anger against her father simmered. Her hands trembled, and she dared not look at Étienne again or she would betray her intense feelings, both her attraction to him and her abhorrence at seeing him forced to play such a menial role.

Rawley and Young vied for her attention, and she wondered if her neck would be sore tomorrow from all its turning back and forth. Mrs. Bane, who sat on Young's right, inquired about the delicate china, and Letitia was glad for the distraction.

"Yes, it was my mother's wedding gift from an aunt."

"It's very pleasing," said Mrs. Bane, holding up her teacup. "Now, your mother was a Chamberlain, wasn't she?"

"Yes," Letitia replied.

"That's right. Her father was a doctor, I recall."

"That's correct."

"And the Hunter family, they go back a long way," Mrs. Bane said.

"There've been Hunters around here for a long time," Mr. Young agreed.

"Yes," said Letitia. "My great-grandfather started the saw-mill. His family had all been sailors and traders, but Great-Grandfather decided to build a career in lumber."

"Smart move," Rawley said. "This area has grown constantly in the last fifty years. Always new buildings going up."

When the main course had been served, Étienne took up his post by the kitchen door, watching the table. Letitia knew he was waiting for a signal from her or her father that something was needed.

She tried not to let her gaze linger on him but noticed that the color in his face was a bit deeper than usual. He must be embarrassed, but he was keeping his dignity.

"I hear there'll be quite a cultural program at Colby College in Waterville next week," Mrs. Bane said.

"Yes, I heard about it," said Rawley. He smiled at Letitia. "Lectures on several topics and musical performances."

"They've a pianist coming all the way from Vienna," said Mrs. Bane.

Rawley nodded. "There's even talk of the city building an opera house. That would be quite an addition for Waterville."

"Don't know as I'd care for opera." Mr. Young shook his head.

"Well, they're also having a brass quintet perform," Mrs. Bane said. "You'd like that, I daresay. Stirring music."

Letitia saw a gleam strike in Mr. Young's eyes. He opened his mouth, but before he could speak, Rawley jumped in.

"As a matter of fact, Miss Hunter, I was planning to invite you to attend the lecture series with me. Or, if you prefer, one of the concerts."

Mr. Young glared at Rawley but spoke to Letitia. "I'd take you round to one of the concerts, Miss Hunter, if you like music."

Letitia looked from one man to the other, feeling a bit like a mouse hesitating between a cat and a mousetrap. She cleared her throat.

"Thank you, gentlemen. That's very kind of you both. I. . . shall have to speak to my father and see what his plans are. He. . .may have already spoken for tickets."

Mrs. Warren, seated to Rawley's left, joined the discussion then. "Oh, I can hardly wait to hear the lecture on women's suffrage. Are you attending that one, Mrs. Bane?"

The lady opposite her coughed. "My husband prefers that

we go to the talk on Amazonian explorations."

The gentlemen chuckled, and Mrs. Bane shrugged, as though she was resigned to missing the lecture that most attracted her.

At that moment, Étienne reached silently to remove Rawley's plate. Letitia caught her breath. Had Rawley even registered the identity of the butler? He began to gently tease Mrs. Bane about her desire to vote, and she replied with good humor.

Letitia swallowed hard and leaned back a little so that Étienne had easy access to her plate, although she'd eaten only half her portion of roast beef and vegetables.

"Mademoiselle is finished?" He whispered near her ear, and a tingle shot all the way down her spine.

"Yes."

She pressed her lips tightly together and stared at his big, muscular hands as he lifted the delicate china. He really was an excellent manservant. But then, he was good at anything he put his mind to. Put him in flannel and give him an ax, and he would chop trees all day. Dress him in wool serge and give him a ledger, and he became the consummate business clerk. In servants' livery. . . No! She hated the very idea of him bowing and performing menial tasks for the likes of John Rawley.

She looked up and found Rawley watching her with hooded eyes.

"Am I correct in assuming this is your first dinner party as hostess?"

She dropped her gaze to the tablecloth. "Yes. Father has not liked to entertain much since my mother died."

"It's going quite well," he assured her with a smile.

"Thank you."

"The only thing that would make it better is if you would tell me you'd accept my invitation."

"I. . .cannot promise that."

"Surely your father wouldn't reserve tickets for the entire series without telling you."

She knew it was true. In fact, her father probably wouldn't

take tickets for any of the lectures or performances. He would consider it a waste of time. But she had no other excuse, and she feared it would sound scandalously rude to refuse simply because she did not want to go with the person issuing the invitation.

"I. . .shall write you a note when I know of his plans."

She could hardly wait until the dessert was served, when she could escape the dining room and avoid the men for a while.

Étienne and Agnes served the cake flawlessly, and Étienne circled the table once more to refill the water glasses and pour coffee for those who wanted it.

At last it was time for the ladies to withdraw to the parlor. Letitia knew her father and the other men would linger in the dining room over their coffee. She hoped Father wouldn't allow anyone to smoke in the house. She'd seen a cigar peeking from Mr. Wheaton's breast pocket. Her father had never taken up smoking and considered it a wasteful and dirty habit. But would he deny the privilege to guests he wanted to impress?

She stood, signaling to the women that the moment had come.

The men also jumped up and hastened to hold the ladies' chairs. Rawley shoved his chair back, perhaps farther and harder than was necessary. The resulting soft *thud* was followed by a sharp intake of breath and a crash.

Letitia stared, along with all the others.

Étienne stood a few inches behind Rawley's chair, staring downward in dismay. On the floor, in pieces, lay one of Letitia's mother's china dessert plates.

ten

Étienne glanced toward the boss. Lincoln Hunter scowled at him, and Étienne sensed mental daggers flying across the dining room.

He knelt and reached for the largest pieces of china, not daring to look Letitia's way. He'd done the worst thing possible: embarrassed her. All evening he had wondered if Rawley recognized him when he let him in the front door. Now he was certain. The contractor had timed the shove of his chair on purpose.

"Sorry," Rawley said.

"Don't mention it." Letitia's quiet reply sounded a bit strained.

Rawley chuckled. "So hard to get well-trained domestic staff these days."

Étienne continued retrieving slivers of china, not expecting Rawley to speak to him. His offhand apology was to the hostess, as was proper.

Agnes darted in from the kitchen with a small broom and dustpan, and Étienne took it from her with a grateful smile.

"Merci."

"The snobbish oaf," Agnes whispered under her breath.

Letitia left the dining room with the ladies following her. Étienne kept busy sweeping up the fragments, his face down.

When he got to the kitchen, Mrs. Watkins was waiting. "Well, now. What did I tell you?"

Étienne winced. "At least I did not spill the soup."

The gray-haired woman scowled, her hands on her hips. "One of the mistress's best plates. I expect Mr. Hunter will take that out of your wages."

He gulped. "Yes, madame. How much?"

"I don't know. That china is probably irreplaceable now."

Étienne sighed. Perhaps he would receive nothing for this evening's work and humiliation.

"Shall I see if the gentlemen want more coffee now?"

Mrs. Watkins exhaled sharply in a near snort. "Can I trust you with the good coffeepot?"

As he reentered the dining room, Étienne's eyes watered. Smoke. Several of the men were puffing on cigars. Mr. Hunter was not partaking but was leaning back, relaxed, in his chair. He beckoned, and Étienne squared his shoulders and approached him.

"We're all set, Steve. Just leave the pot and go help Mrs. Watkins clean up now. And see me before you leave."

Étienne nodded and went back to the kitchen.

Mrs. Watkins frowned at him. "They want something?"

"No, madame. I am yours to command now. What would you have me do?"

She opened a drawer and pulled out a piece of white linen. When she shook it out, he saw that it was a large apron.

"The water is hot for the dishes."

Étienne nodded. "Yes, madame." He removed his suit jacket and hung it on a peg near the back door, then put the apron on, tying it behind his waist.

Mrs. Watkins turned to Agnes. "Go and check on the ladies. See if they want anything."

Étienne rolled up his sleeves, poured the hot water into the dishpan, and swished the soap into it. This was not so bad. He always did dishes at home when he was a boy. He began to hum under his breath as he eased a stack of china plates into the water.

"Be careful now!"

He nodded at Mrs. Watkins's admonition, and she smiled. "Agnes told me it wasn't your fault, but likely that won't matter to Mr. Hunter."

"It's all right."

She shook her head. "You're a good lad, and I'll tell Mr. Hunter so."

"I do not want him to regret giving me this job," Étienne said.

"There now. Just you wash up those dishes and don't drop anything more, and that will show him you're not clumsy. Mr. Hunter never could abide a clumsy person." She brought him a clean dishrag, and Étienne was ready to pitch in to his task feeling a little less an outcast.

"Oh, and we'll need more hot water," Mrs. Watkins said. "Take these two pails out to the pump and fill them, please."

He took the two buckets she indicated and went out the back door. Earlier, the cook had shown him the attached shed that housed the pitcher pump. He worked the handle vigorously, glad to have a brief physical outlet for his frustration.

When he plodded back through the kitchen door balancing the full buckets, he was surprised to see Letitia in conference with Mrs. Watkins.

"It's not a problem as far as I'm concerned, Miss Letitia. The lad is sorry he caused a scene, but it really wasn't his fault, you know. Ask Agnes. But he's willing to accept blame; he told me so himself." The cook looked at him, and he nodded gravely, then poured the buckets of water slowly into the reservoir on the stove. He could feel Letitia's gaze on him, but he didn't turn toward her. It would not bode well if the cook thought the hired servant had designs on the master's daughter.

Letitia left a moment later, casting one confused glance over her shoulder as she opened the door to the hallway. Étienne sighed and placed the last clean plate in the rack beside him. Agnes breezed in carrying a tray of dirty cups.

"Here you go! I'll dry."

She snatched up a linen towel and began to wipe the clean dishes so fast he had to hurry to keep up with her. But his every movement was precise and deliberate, and no more accidents befell the china.

❧

When the gentlemen joined the ladies in the parlor, it was all Letitia could do to keep from glaring at her father. Despite Mrs. Watkins's reassurances, her father's arrogance appalled her. Shame on him for requiring Étienne to do this!

Rawley picked up a cushioned Queen Anne side chair and carried it over to place it by the love seat where Letitia was perched with Mrs. Wheaton.

She gave him a faint smile and returned to her conversation. Rawley soon found an opening, however, and she was forced to include him.

He leaned toward her when no one else was listening and said, "Tell me, has your father always been a teetotaler? I expected he'd bring out the brandy after dinner, but not so."

She frowned at him. "Why would you expect that? My father has never been a drinker."

"Ah. I do wish you'd go out with me, Letitia. I could show you places where we could get good food and drink. Nothing overpowering, just a fine, light wine to complement the meal. I'm sure you'd see how it adds to a special dinner."

Aghast, she watched him for a moment from beneath her eyelashes. What sort of response could she give to that? At last she said softly, "I consider that an insult to this family's hospitality, sir."

He sat back with a smile. "No offense intended."

She saw that Mrs. Bane was examining the knickknacks on the mantelpiece.

"Excuse me." She jumped up and hurried across the room. "Do you collect Dresden figures, Mrs. Bane? My mother was enamored of these."

During the next hour, she avoided Rawley as much as possible and gently but firmly told Mr. Young she was not interested in attending a family reunion with him. At last the guests began to leave. Étienne helped them with their wraps in the hallway, and Letitia stood at her father's side, thanking them all for attending and wishing them a safe journey home.

When the last one was out the door, her father turned to Étienne. "There are a few dishes yet in the parlor, Steve."

"I will get them, sir."

Étienne went into the parlor, and Letitia grasped her father's arm as he started toward his study. "How could you do this to him?" she hissed.

He frowned and eyed her hand on his sleeve austerely. "Whatever are you talking about?"

"You've humiliated Mr. LeClair."

He stared down at her for a moment. "I thought you understood my feelings about LeClair."

A huge lump popped up in Letitia's throat.

"Steve will do whatever he is paid to do," her father said sternly. "And you, my dear, should mind your own business." He turned and walked down the hallway, disappearing into his study.

Letitia stood rooted to the hall carpet. Her chest and throat ached, and tears filled her eyes. She blinked them back and walked to the stairs but stopped with her foot on the bottom step.

It wasn't right!

She raised her chin and went back to the parlor door. Étienne was about to emerge, carrying a tray with several cups and glasses on it. He stopped and stood facing her, the tray between them. His large brown eyes were cautious, and perhaps a bit sad.

"I am so sorry, Étienne! My father should not have forced you to do this. I hope you do not think that I consider you to be a servant. You are a skilled clerk, and you should be treated with more respect."

She paused for breath, and Étienne smiled. "It's all right, Letitia."

He pronounced her name with his soft French accent, giving it a gentle, flowing lilt. Her heart fluttered. She closed her eyes for a moment, unable to resist imagining what it would be like to be loved by this man, to hear him utter soft, sweet words of love in her ear.

"I do not mind being in a position of service," he went on, and Letitia opened her eyes.

"You. . .don't?"

"No. I came here to serve your father."

"In the office, yes, but after hours you shouldn't have to—"

"Uh-uh," he said quietly. "Mr. Hunter did not force me to do this."

"He didn't?"

Étienne's smile broadened, and her heart thumped.

"Not at all, so be at peace. If there is anything else I can do to make your life and your father's go more smoothly, I would be happy to oblige."

"But—" She looked down at the tray he carried. "This is not part of your job."

"No, you are correct. This is extra. But it is well, mademoiselle. Please do not distress yourself over it."

Stunned, Letitia watched him carry the tray down the long hall to the kitchen door. When it closed behind him, she strode to the entrance of her father's den. He was seated at the old oak rolltop desk that had been his grandfather's, staring up at her mother's portrait on the wall between the windows.

"Ah, Letitia, I thought you went upstairs."

"Not yet."

"Is there something I can do for you?"

"It's about Mr. LeClair."

He swung around to face her, scowling. "I told you to keep out of it."

"I know you did, but. . .Father, I thought you made him come here tonight and pretend to be our butler, perhaps to embarrass me."

"Certainly not."

"Then why did you ask him to do it? I hope it was not some

haughty notion of keeping him in his place."

He barked a short laugh. "All right, missy, you sit down and listen to me."

Letitia gulped and sat down one of the comfortable, leather-covered chairs. "Yes, Father?"

"A few days ago, I mentioned the dinner party to Steve at the office. You were gone somewhere—to the bank, I think. Anyway, Mrs. Watkins needed a helper for the evening, and I instructed Steve to find someone to take the job. I asked him to find a clever fellow in the French quarter who could look handsome, be polite, and work hard one evening for some extra cash."

Letitia opened her mouth, then closed it.

Her father picked up the silver pen that lay on his desk. "Later that day, Steve approached me and inquired—a bit nervously, I admit—if I would consider him eligible for the job, as he would appreciate the chance to earn some extra money."

Letitia gasped.

"What—you don't believe it?"

"I. . ." She frowned, unable to meet his gaze.

"Steve comes from a poor family. You know that, don't you?"

She nodded.

"Letitia," her father's voice softened. "My dear, they are poverty-stricken. But Steve is a strong and clever young man. When he sees an opportunity to help his poor widowed mother and the younger children, he takes it. And that day he saw such an opportunity. I gave him money for a new collar and tie and told him to show up early to help Mrs. Watkins set up, then show the guests in. He did very well tonight, I thought, except for that one little mishap. But you see, Steve is a working-class man. I've enabled him to rise to a clerk's position. Well and good. But he still sees a need to earn extra money, so I allowed him to do that. Do you understand, Letitia?"

"Understand what, Father?"

"He is beneath you, but he is capable of defending himself. He doesn't need you to fight his battles for him. And I do not like to see you so overset by this imagined wrong."

Letitia rose and walked to the door. She turned around and looked at her father, but his eyes were hard and unyielding. She hurried out the door and up the stairs.

Halfway up, she stopped. Her mind reeled with retorts she ought to have made. If he paid Étienne the same wage he had paid Weston, for instance, then Étienne wouldn't need to kowtow to their guests for extra money. And if Father truly valued Étienne as he said he did, he would see that such a man would be an excellent choice for his daughter. Such a man would always take care of the woman he loved.

She set her jaw, determined to storm back down the stairs and launch another argument. She would not back down. She would show him that he was wrong about Étienne's station and that people could move from one plane in life to another.

She took one step, and the kitchen door opened.

Étienne came down the hallway whistling. He stopped walking when he saw her on the stairs, and his whistle silenced. They looked at each other for a long moment, and then he smiled.

Letitia's pulse careened in her veins. She smiled back but knew she was close to tears.

"Your party went well," he said.

She winced. "I'm glad it's over. The ladies were all nice to me, but. . ." She saw that his face had taken on an anxiety, with tiny lines creasing his forehead, where she could barely see the mysterious scar. "Father explained the situation to me. I'm sorry I made a fuss about it. I hope I haven't added to your discomfort."

"I am fine, mademoiselle."

"Well, I do hope Father doesn't make you pay for the damaged plate. That was not your fault."

His expression lightened. "As a matter of fact, he left my

wages with Mrs. Watkins, and she just gave them to me. The full amount he promised."

She sighed. "That's good. I was afraid. . . Oh, Étienne, I'm sorry. I was certain Father was making you do this, and I wondered if you hated doing it."

"No, no, it did not bother me one bit. And the money I earned this evening, I will send it home to my mother. That makes me very happy, to be able to help her more than usual."

Letitia nodded. "I suppose it's somewhat like the way I feel about helping Father with the business. Only better because Father doesn't really need me. He could hire someone else."

He was watching her with those large, chocolate brown eyes, and she stopped, wondering if she sounded silly. She realized how tired she was. This was probably not the best time to try to analyze her relationship with her father.

"I will tell you one thing that makes me happy," he said.

"Please do." His smile sent a thrill through her.

"Seeing you, Letitia. Seeing you here in your home. You were a very good and beautiful hostess tonight, and your guests had a pleasant evening."

"Thank you. I hope I didn't embarrass you by my reaction when I saw you. . .working tonight."

"Not at all. I was afraid I was the one who brought the mortification to you."

"No, please don't think that."

He glanced down the hallway. "I'm glad we've had this chance to speak to each other."

"So am I. Perhaps sometime we will have another opportunity, and you can tell me more about your family."

He nodded. "I would like that."

A rattling of pans came faintly from the kitchen, and they both looked down the hall and then back at each other.

Étienne held out his hand. Letitia hesitated, then leaned over the railing and clasped it. She tried not to recall her father's adamant words: *I thought you understood my feelings about LeClair.*

"I must go," he all but whispered. "Perhaps I shall see you at church tomorrow."

"Yes."

They stood gazing at each other for another long moment, and her pulse cavorted wildly. Then he gave a nod, as though he completely understood her chaotic feelings, and turned to leave.

Letitia scurried up to her bedchamber, thankful that her father had not emerged from his study while Étienne stood holding her hand over the stair railing. She shut her door and leaned against it, breathing in broken gasps. She ought not to have confronted her father. Had she done Étienne irreparable harm by letting her father see her anger at the perceived slight? Could her father read her other emotions as well? Did he guess the depth of the attraction she felt for Étienne? Could he see that love was growing in her heart, and that she could not stop it?

A soft knock sounded on the door, and Letitia jumped away from it.

"Yes?"

Agnes's voice came through the panels. "May I help you with your dress, Miss Letitia?"

"Thank you. I'd appreciate that."

The stress of the party and her anxiety for Étienne had drained her strength. Having the maid on hand to assist her was a relief, and she allowed Agnes to undo her buttons, lift the dress over her head, and bring her a robe. Then she sat down and let the girl take down her hair and brush it with soothing strokes.

"Your hair is so pretty, Miss Letitia." Agnes smiled at her in the mirror.

"Thank you."

"Mrs. Watkins says two of the men who were here tonight want to marry you."

Letitia was too tired to even consider blushing. "I wouldn't say that. I hardly know them."

"Well, the blond man was handsome. I'd marry him if he learned some manners. If he asked me, of course."

"Would you?"

"Oh, yes, miss. He's very rich, I think."

"Well, money isn't everything, you know."

"Yes, I do know, but it helps."

Letitia smiled. "Did you enjoy working here today?"

"Oh, yes! I'd like to work here all the time. Was I. . .all right?"

"You did fine. I'll keep you in mind if my father is of a mind to hire anyone."

"Of course, you know who the most handsome man here tonight was, don't you?" Agnes asked with a roguish smile.

"No, who? My father?"

A laugh burbled from the girl's throat. "No, although he cuts a very distinguished figure. I was speaking of Mr. LeClair." A dreamy look came over Agnes's face. "I suppose he's too old for me."

Letitia twisted around to look at her. *Agnes mustn't be more than seventeen,* she judged. *And Étienne must be. . .what, five and twenty?* Agnes's admiration of him was slightly disturbing, but even worse was the thought that every young woman in the French quarter was probably languishing over him. "I should think he is."

Agnes sighed. "I was afraid of that. I liked him excessively."

eleven

At the end of August, Lincoln Hunter announced over breakfast his intention of viewing the site of the new sawmill on the west bank of the Kennebec River in Fairfield. He would stay at a hotel and go over the new mill with the builder and the man he had chosen as its foreman.

"I'll take LeClair with me," he told Letitia as he perused his morning newspaper.

Letitia's heart caught. She wondered if she could persuade him to take her, too. But, no, he would want her to keep the office running smoothly.

"After that, we'll take the train to Bangor," her father continued, "and run up to check on things at the camps."

Her hopes plummeted. A tour of Northern's lumber camps meant that her father and Étienne would be gone for several weeks. She should have expected it; he'd been fretting over the new bunkhouse being built five miles north of the Spruce Run Camp, wondering if it would be ready for the crew who would arrive after the first hard frost. It was like her father to want to inspect the preparations personally. Letitia knew he had a reputation as an exacting employer, but one who provided good conditions for his laborers.

"I suppose this is the best time to go," she said.

"I think so. We'll be busy this fall, and I won't be able to get away. And if there's anything amiss up there, I want to know it now."

In the office, Letitia waited all morning for her father to call Étienne aside and tell him. Nearly two months had passed since the dinner party, and her friendship with Étienne had progressed gradually until the bond was stronger than any she had ever known outside family. He felt it, too; she was certain. But they both knew it could go no further, and with unspoken agreement they did not seek to change that. At church on Sundays, they smiled and spoke to each other. On the occasions when her father left the office for a short time, they had quiet, contented conversations. They were learning more about each other, and Letitia's heart leaped each day when she walked into the office and met Étienne's charming smile. Still, she knew this was as deep as the relationship could go. She would not think beyond the present.

By noon, her father still had not confided his plans to Étienne, and tension built in Letitia's heart. They walked home for lunch, leaving Étienne at the office, and sat down to the meal Mrs. Watkins had prepared.

Letitia bowed her head briefly and offered a silent prayer. She'd asked Father once, shortly after her mother died, why he no longer asked the blessing at meals, and he had replied, "If you want to pray, then pray." Since then, she had not mentioned it.

"You'd best start packing for me this afternoon," he said, cutting the slice of ham on his plate. "I expect to be gone three or four weeks."

"Have you told Mr. LeClair yet, Father?" She had taken portions of each dish but was finding it difficult to eat.

"Haven't mentioned it yet. Thought I'd tell him Monday."

"But, Father, he'll need time to prepare, too."

Lincoln held up his cup, and Letitia rose to fill it with coffee. "It won't take him long to pack a bag."

"But. . .just as a courtesy. . ."

"You tell him," her father said with a shrug. "If you think it's important, let him know this afternoon. We leave Wednesday."

"You don't want to tell him yourself? What if he has questions?"

"I'm meeting Russell Chandler at 1:30 in his office. What kind of questions would LeClair have?"

"I don't know. What do you want him to take?"

"Paper and pen, the things he uses for accounting and correspondence. And his personal things, of course."

"All right. I'll tell him."

"Forgot to give you the payroll this morning," her father said. "It's on my desk. You can take it to the bank after lunch. I'm raising LeClair's salary two dollars a week."

She nodded without a word, but her heart sang.

"What?" he asked, looking at her shrewdly.

"Nothing."

"You're thinking it's high time."

"I didn't say that."

"Well, he's become very dependable, and I told him I'd raise his wage this summer."

Her father had entrusted Mark Warren, his friend and attorney, with care of Letitia during his absence before, so she wasn't surprised when he said, "If you need anything while I'm gone, see Mr. Warren. And charge your groceries and such." He pulled out his wallet and laid a five-dollar bill on the table. "That enough for your sundries while I'm away?"

"Plenty, I'm sure."

"All right. If you need more, ask at the bank. You will be in my place, Letitia. The foremen will come to you with their headaches, as they would to me. I trust you to use your judgment, and do call on Mr. Warren if an urgent situation arises."

"Yes, Father." Letitia was confident she could handle the office while he was away. Last summer, he'd taken Mr. Weston with him on a two-week trip, leaving her in charge, and she'd had no major difficulties. Of course, it was understood that she was to put off any major decisions until her father's return.

Her father left her at the corner of the street that led to the office and went on alone to his appointment. When Letitia opened the door at Northern Lumber, Étienne was speaking to the mill supervisor, Raymond Linden.

"Mr. Hunter won't be back for a while," he told Linden. "Perhaps another hour."

The man sighed. "I've got a broken belt on the saw, and I wanted to tell Mr. Hunter. We're getting it laced up as quickly as we can, but we'll run a mite behind this afternoon."

"I'll tell him," LeClair promised.

"I'll have things right again soon," Linden pledged. He nodded at Letitia and went out the door.

Étienne looked at her then dropped his gaze. "Letitia," he murmured.

"Étienne." Their quiet greetings when her father was absent always thrilled her, and she stepped to her father's desk to get the papers he had left there. She knew that if she looked Étienne in the eye again, her joy, tempered by the knowledge that he would soon be leaving for an extended period of time, would show. When she walked back to her desk, he had turned back to his own work. She sat down and cleared her throat. He swung around at once.

"My father asked me to tell you. . ."

His dark eyes widened in inquiry, and she looked away. Those beautiful, sympathetic eyes were far too distracting.

"He'll be leaving on a business trip next Wednesday, and you will accompany him."

"Where are we going?"

"To Fairfield, where the new mill is under construction. Father may have lined up some other appointments as well in the Waterville area. He wants you to do the accounting and correspondence for him."

Étienne nodded.

"And after that—" His eyebrows arched, and she broke off, dismayed as her pulse rate increased.

"After?"

"He plans to tour the lumber camps up north."

"And. . .I'll be with him?"

"Yes." She wondered what was going through his mind,

behind the dark eyes. He lowered his gaze to the floor, and she noticed that his dark lashes lay against his cheek. She turned away quickly.

"Have you taken your lunch yet?" she asked.

"No." He stood up and turned toward the door, then paused. "Do you suppose—?"

"What?" she ventured.

"It was just a thought. That I might be able to visit my family."

"Perhaps," Letitia said. "You could ask him."

He nodded and strode toward the door with a new purpose in his walk.

When he was gone, she felt apprehensive. She would be alone in the office for up to a month. Étienne would go with her father to act as his secretary and handle the details of his travel. But he was homesick and would soon be on the Quebec border far to the north, closer to his homeland than to Zimmerville. Lincoln Hunter had brought Étienne back from the camps on his last trip. Would he come back alone this time?

❧

In the first four days of the journey, Étienne's list of new experiences grew rapidly. After their tour of the half-finished sawmill, he drove on to the city of Waterville with the boss, where they stayed in a hotel. Mr. Hunter took a suite on the ground floor, and Étienne expected he might be billeted in a small room on the third story, or even at a boardinghouse in a poorer section of town. But, no, the boss informed him that the second bedroom of the suite was for him. He was to stay nearby so that he would be handy to write a letter anytime Mr. Hunter took a notion to dictate one.

The room's opulence shocked Étienne. It was three times the size of the one he occupied in the Ouellettes' home, and the curtains and linens were the finest quality he'd ever seen, outside the Hunter home. The paintings on the walls and matching china pitchers and bowls in the bedrooms must have cost a fortune.

After luncheon in the hotel dining room, the boss visited an architect and a contractor, and Étienne took notes and wrote out a large order for the contractor. When they returned to the hotel, Mr. Hunter instructed him to prepare the envelope for the order and mail it to Letitia.

"Do you wish me to write anything to Miss Hunter?" Étienne asked.

"Oh, whatever you think is appropriate." Hunter took out his pocket watch. "I'm going to stop by city hall and see an old friend for a few minutes. I won't need you. You can catch up your paperwork while I'm gone."

Étienne sat at the walnut secretary in the suite's sitting room to prepare the letter. He addressed the envelope first. *Northern Lumber* would do, he knew, but it pleased him to commit her name to paper, so he penned *Miss Letitia Hunter* above the company's name. He said it aloud. "Miss Letitia Hunter." It almost hurt to say it. He finished the address and took a sheet of paper.

Dear. . .

Just writing that one word and knowing to whom it was going set his heart tripping. He took a deep breath and continued writing.

Dear Miss Hunter,

*   Enclosed is the order Mr. Hunter procured from Mr. Orcutt of Waterville Builders. I trust you and the staff will have no trouble in fulfilling this order and having the lumber delivered by rail to Mr. Orcutt.*

He hesitated then concluded the note:

Very truly yours,
Étienne LeClair (for Mr. Hunter)

He decided it would do. Businesslike. A touch more cordial than was absolutely necessary, but not so much that it would raise the boss's eyebrows if he should see it. How he wished he could set down his true feelings for her to read.

My dearest Letitia,

We have been several days on the road, and already I miss you more than I can say. My thoughts are with you, my darling, as I picture you sitting at your desk, so poised and competent, yet so lovely, with your vibrant blue eyes and—

The door opened abruptly. "Say, Steve."

He jumped from his chair. "Yes, Mr. Hunter?"

"When you go out to post that order, perhaps you should shop for another suit. It's been uncommonly hot this week."

Étienne swallowed hard. He'd sent most of his last paycheck to Quebec and had brought along only a couple of dollars for pocket money on the trip.

"Sir?"

Mr. Hunter shrugged. "Up to you, but that black must be stifling in the sun. There's a decent haberdashery down on Water Street that could probably meet your needs. Something lighter. A linen jacket and trousers, maybe."

Étienne couldn't help staring as the boss opened his wallet and extracted a ten-dollar bill.

"Here. We're having lunch tomorrow with the mayor and his wife. I told him I have a bright young man in my employ with me, and he said to bring you along. You'll have a chance to meet a young fellow who's just taken a seat on the city council. Educational for you."

"Yes. . .sir."

Hunter held out the money. "Well, take it. It's a business expense."

"Thank you, sir." Étienne wondered if this would be deducted from his pay later, but Mr. Hunter hinted at no such thing.

"If you have any change, put it toward socks and collars and such. A man in business has to dress the part."

Étienne nodded and folded the bill into his breast pocket.

"If you look successful, men expect you'll give good service and help them be successful."

"Yes, sir."

Hunter nodded. "Good."

"Did you. . .wish to see the letter, sir?"

"Letter? What letter?"

"To Miss Hunter."

"Oh, no, that's all right. Just send it right out so she'll get it tomorrow. Orcutt wants that order in a hurry, and I assured him we had everything in stock. Linden can have it to him in two days, I'd say."

"Oh, yes, sir, I think so."

Two hours later, Étienne returned to the hotel wearing a new suit and a hat much the same style as the one Mr. Hunter wore. He felt overdressed, but none of the gentlemen in the hotel lobby stared at him.

The suite was quiet, but the door to Mr. Hunter's room stood partway open. Étienne approached it and peeked in. The boss was stretched out on the bed, snoring softly.

For two more days they stayed in town. Mr. Hunter seemed to do more socializing than business, yet each day he gleaned one or two large orders for the firm. Étienne gained a new respect for the boss. He'd half expected Mr. Hunter to cut up when out from under his daughter's eye, but the boss maintained his conservative routine: early to bed, early to rise, a brisk morning walk, three square meals a day, and no alcohol or tobacco, though his friends and clients offered them routinely.

On the fourth day, they took the train north. Étienne sat upright in the seat, alert to the swaying sensation, the warm breeze flowing through the windows, the smoke that hung in the air, and the people around him. It was only his second railroad journey, and he found it slightly scary but exciting. Mr.

Hunter sat by the window and was already slumped in his seat with his eyes closed, but Étienne knew he could not sleep as long as the train was moving. The trip to Bangor would only last two hours, and he didn't want to miss anything.

He wondered what Letitia was doing. No doubt she was at the office by now. Would the boss make any appointments in Bangor, or would they head right out to the lumber camps? Étienne hoped he would see a few businessmen, so there would be another order to send to Letitia that afternoon. The notes he enclosed with those orders were the high point of his day. Knowing she would read them in a day or two was better than lunch at the mayor's house, better than fancy new clothes, better even than feeling that the boss was pleased with him.

The train began to slow, and the conductor came down the aisle.

"Bangor! Next stop Bangor!"

Étienne closed his eyes for a moment. He was perhaps fifty miles away from her now and would soon be farther. The trip was exciting, and the possibility of visiting his family was sweet. He'd dared to mention it to the boss this morning, and Mr. Hunter had not said no. He'd only said, "We'll see how things are when we get to Little North Fork Camp." Étienne knew that was the camp closest to the Quebec border.

But, as much as he longed to see his mother and siblings, already he was looking forward to returning to Zimmerville. His heart lay southward, with Letitia.

twelve

The day following Mr. Hunter and Étienne's train ride, Letitia received a thick packet of papers from Waterville along with the regular daily mail. She sat down to open the envelope addressed in Étienne's hand.

On top was a note in her father's scrawl:

> Met with Langley & Fortin today. They want 5,000 bd. ft. pine. LeClair will write it up for you. Add another 500 ft. red oak to Orcutt's order. Saw the mayor yesterday. Hope all is well at the office.
>
> Yr loving father,
> LH

Letitia sighed. Her father was no doubt widening his circle of political acquaintances. He believed in the power of lobbying for the lumber industry. She set the note aside and examined the papers that came with it. In Étienne's neat handwriting were the new orders. There was also a new schedule of lumber prices. At the bottom he had written:

> Miss H.,
> I hope this information will aid you in preparing the orders. It came this morning from New York.
>
> Wishing you good health,
> E. LeClair

Letitia couldn't help comparing the two messages. Despite his affectionate closing, her father's note seemed less empathetic than Étienne's.

She looked bleakly across the room at his empty chair and longed to see him sitting there once more. But he and her father must be on their way to the lumber camps already.

The door swung open, and Jacques Laplante entered.

"Bon matin, ma petite. Comment vas-tu?"

"Bien, Jacques." She smiled up at the big man, knowing that if she had a real emergency she would run to Jacques long before calling on Mark Warren. *"J'ai une lettre de mon père,"* she said, gesturing toward the papers on her desk.

"Bien."

"I'll send him a note at Little North Fork to let him know how things are going here."

"I came to tell you we have exceeded our goal for production this week, and I am calling for the bonus your father authorized."

"What bonus?"

"He tol' me before he left that if the Henshaw order was finished before Friday to give the men two dollars bonus. They have been driving themselves hard all week."

"He didn't tell me."

Jacques frowned. "He should have. Maybe he didn't think they could do it. Is it agreeable?"

"Well, if Father said so."

"It was Étienne's idea. He tol' your papa a fortnight ago that to get the men to work harder he needs to promise them something extra. And your papa really wanted that order out of the way. My crew is loading it on the cars now."

"Fine. If you tell me it's so, I believe it."

Jacques nodded. "You are lonesome while your papa is away?"

"No more than usual," she said, wishing she hadn't let slip that insight into her inner life.

Jacques looked closely at her. "You come to supper with Angelique and me."

"Oh, that's all right. I'm fine."

"No, you come. You haven't been to the house for a while. We will tell stories and drink tea and talk."

She smiled. With people like Jacques and Angelique nearby, loneliness was a choice. "All right. I'd like that."

She wrote a letter to her father after lunch, detailing the business that had come in and noting that she had authorized Jacques to pay out a bonus to the crew. If her father didn't like it, it was too late, and she would bear his wrath.

After some consideration, she took another sheet of paper.

Mr. LeClair,

I hope you don't mind I rifled your desk today for the address to Adirondack Lumber. It was urgent, or I would not have done so. I trust your trip has been comfortable so far.

She hesitated then wrote:

I do hope you are able to visit your family.

Sincerely,
Letitia Hunter

She sat looking at the paper for several minutes, then folded it with shaking hands, sealed it, and wrote on the front: *Mr. E. LeClair.*

After a moment's thought, she took the letter to her father and at the bottom wrote: *P.S. If it is convenient, I believe Mr. LeClair desires to visit his family in Quebec when you are near the border.*

She didn't know if she would hear from her father again, as mail was sporadic at best north of Bangor. She posted the letters before the afternoon train left for Bangor, including a couple of business documents in the packet, then plunged back into her work, trying not to think about the note she had sent LeClair. Would he think her forward to send him an unnecessary personal note?

Just three days later, she sat staring at a letter in Étienne's handwriting. She put off opening it, trying to calm the jitters that seized her every time she looked at her name, *Miss Letitia Hunter*, written in his neat script on the envelope.

It's only business, she told herself, but as long as she didn't open it, there was no proof of that. She recalled their talks on the few occasions when they'd been alone in the office and the smiles that were meant only for her.

She waited until the lunch hour, locked the door, and slit the envelope. The first sheet was a full-page letter, not a hasty note.

Dear Miss Letitia,
I hope I do not offend by addressing you thus.

Letitia's heart lurched. This was more than a business letter.

Your father requests that I inform you he is in good health and has had a profitable journey so far, as the enclosed orders will attest. Production for these orders may begin as soon as Mr. Linden is prepared.

She ruffled the enclosures, noting three new orders. Apparently her father had stopped over a day in Bangor and made good use of his time. She turned back to the letter and sat very still, looking at the words, so neat, so ordinary—to her so significant.

I have broached to your father the subject of visiting my family. He seems open to this, so long as I swear to rejoin him quickly. I think perhaps he fears I will not want to return to Zimmerville. I assured him I will not desert him, and he has given me permission to take three days leave while he is at Little North Fork Camp, if all goes smoothly.

Letitia smiled. Trust her father to leave himself a loophole.

I write this in the train station at Bangor and have only a few minutes before we go beyond frequent mail service. I hope you do not take offense if I say I think of you and pray often for you, for your safekeeping in the absence of your father.

Sincerely,
Étienne LeClair

Letitia closed her eyes and breathed deeply. Before opening them, she prayed, *Lord, thank You. Keep them safe. And if it is in Your plan, please allow this friendship to continue to grow.*

Raymond Linden came to the office that afternoon, and she gave him the specifications for the new orders.

"We might need to hire a couple of extra men to get these out before we finish the Rawley order," he said, eyeing the paper.

"Fine. I know Father wants the entire mill's production available for Rawley when the oak arrives."

"Well, we've put through the spruce," Linden said. "It's in the drying shed. But when the rest comes in, we need to concentrate on that."

She nodded. "There should be men looking for work now."

"All right. I'll put one crew on this Hatcher order tomorrow."

Letitia worked in solitude through the afternoon, interrupted occasionally by customers. At five o'clock, she closed the office and went home. It was hot, and she opened the windows. Mrs. Watkins had left her supper in the icebox, but she wasn't very hungry. She stood before the open parlor window, overlooking the town that sprawled between the house and the river. The wind lifted strands of her dark hair, and she began taking out the pins that held her bun firmly on the back of her head.

If she were truly an independent businesswoman, she would change into a fashionable dress and go out to eat supper at a restaurant. That was what Mrs. Harris, the owner of the emporium, did. The people of Zimmerville watched her in confusion. The matrons asked each other why Mrs. Harris didn't take another husband. Any one of a number of well-off bachelors or widowers would be happy to take care of her.

Letitia's ideas of being cared for were nebulous. Her father took care of her; at least, he provided for her needs. But she knew there were deeper needs that he could never meet.

In her imagination, there was somewhere a man who would want her to make a home for him, to be waiting for him in the evening when he left his work. He would love her deeply and would strive to keep her happy, not just well fed and clothed.

As she took the letter out of her pocket and sat down with it by the lamp, Letitia realized that for the past few months, the imaginary suitor had dark eyes and hair, and the solemn expression of Étienne LeClair.

He was beyond the railhead now. If she sent a letter, it might never reach him. She knew they would be at Little North Fork for several days; her father had granted him three days' leave there. Perhaps if she addressed a letter to him there, it would catch up with them before they went on.

She prayed before she began to write. *Lord, am I putting too much store in this? Please help me not to be indiscreet.*

She sat with the pen poised over the blank paper. The greeting would set the tone. *Dear Étienne?* No, she had been trained to write letters in a more formal style. He had addressed her as Miss Letitia, and she did not want to seem forward.

> *Dear Mr. LeClair,*
> *I received your letter from Bangor with pleasure and have attended to the business referred to therein.*

It sounded stiff, but she let it stand.

> *I am pleased to hear you will be able to visit your home, and I hope this letter will reach you at Little North Fork. Please give my regards to my father, and tell him all is well in the mill and lumberyard.*

Now what? The letter was too short, but she couldn't fill it with empty drivel. She thought back over the last few days, how she had missed his presence in the office and at church.

> *I visited with the Laplantes a few days ago. Friends like Jacques and Angelique are a true gift from God.*

She hesitated then decided to step off into more personal matters. If she did not hear from him, she would know she had probed too deeply.

> *I am wondering, and I hope you do not mind my asking, how you came to know the Lord. Are your family believers as well? If my inquiry is too direct, I beg your pardon.*

Stilted, stilted, stilted.

She reviewed the list of camps her father would be visiting. He would spend only a night or two at most of them.

> *If you receive this, you will be nearly halfway done with your journey. I pray daily for you and my father, and trust to see you again soon.*
>
> > *Yours truly,*
> > *Letitia*

She paused, debating on whether or not she could be casual enough to omit her last name, but lost her courage and penned *Hunter* at the end.

Her heart raced as she addressed the envelope in care of the boss at Little North Fork Camp. She would take the letter to the post office early the next morning and send it off with a prayer, entrusting its delivery to God.

⋅᪣⋅

Étienne settled into the rustic traveling life with ease. He drove Mr. Hunter from one lumber camp to the next and wrote up a report at each, detailing the provisions needed, crews expected to sign on for the season, and preparations for the winter's logging enterprise. He wrote letters to the foremen and cooks for each camp, asking them to confirm their intentions to work for Northern Lumber this year, and he totaled up the many lists of supplies purchased.

Mr. Hunter seemed uncomfortable while the warm weather lasted. A few days after they left Bangor, however, the temperature began to drop and the nights were chilly. The boss regained some energy then, but still Étienne thought he looked drawn. His face had the same grayish cast it had taken on the previous winter. When he wrote to Letitia, as instructed, that her father said he was well, Étienne felt he was not being entirely truthful. He tried to spare Hunter any exertion.

Étienne's quick visit home was bittersweet. His mother and younger siblings were overjoyed to see him but couldn't understand why he had come all that way if he could only stay a short time with them.

He brought them a small sum of money and a couple of books he had purchased in Maine. His mother was proud to hear how highly the boss praised Étienne's education, though he had gotten most of it at the little village school.

"Won't you ever come home to live?" his fifteen-year-old brother, Paul, asked.

"I. . .don't know," Étienne admitted. "Mr. Hunter has raised my wages, and I like what I'm doing now."

"I want to go into the lumber camps this year," said André, who was eighteen.

"Me, too," Paul added.

"Not you," their mother protested. "I need you here, Paul."

Two of Étienne's sisters were married and lived nearby, and they brought their babies over to see him.

In the morning, he was sad to leave them all but glad he'd seen with his own eyes that they were doing all right. His mother admitted that without the money he sent regularly, she and the three children left at home would be hard-pressed.

"But if I am hired this fall," André said, "we won't need your pay anymore. You can come home."

His mother said softly, "Perhaps it is time your brother thought of having a family of his own."

Étienne said nothing, but he couldn't quite meet his mother's penetrating gaze. He pulled her in for a hug, then set on his way. He would walk five miles to the next village, where a farmer had promised him a ride to the next town.

As he walked, his thoughts flew to Zimmerville. How was Letitia faring? Would there be a letter from her awaiting him at the camp? He prayed for her as he traveled, longing for the day when he would see her again.

thirteen

The saws and planers roared without pause, and Letitia was busy in the office every day. She visited the post office each morning, trying to push down the hope that rose repeatedly, until she saw that there was nothing from the north.

By the end of the week, she was certain that she had, after all, been too candid in her last letter. She wished desperately that she had not written it.

By the following Wednesday, she was depressed. If Étienne felt she was pursuing him, he might change his mind and resign. He wouldn't want to work every day with a girl who lacked discretion.

Woman, she told herself. *Not girl.* She was twenty-one, her birthday passing in the middle of the week without remark from anyone. If her father had been at home, she would have made sure they marked the day somehow, even if she had to instigate it. Her mother had always prepared a special meal for birthdays, and her father always brought her something, a trinket, even since her mother's death.

She had spent the evening of her birthday alone, sitting at home with a book—a collection of short stories by Robert Louis Stevenson called *Island Nights Entertainments*. She had seen it in the window of Mrs. Harris's store that morning and had rationalized that if Father were home he would surely buy it for her as a birthday gift.

On Saturday, she made her usual trek to the post office, carrying a sheaf of bills to mail. She had given up on hearing from Étienne again. Maybe her letter had missed him at Little North Fork. . . .

"Miss Hunter!" the postmaster exclaimed when she entered

the tiny post office. "I've been looking for ye. I've got something interesting for ye, sure, this morning."

Letitia's eyes widened as the rotund, white-haired man brought a flat box from beneath the counter and set it down in front of her.

" 'Tis not for Northern Lumber, no, no," he said jovially. " 'Tis addressed to yourself, Miss Letitia Hunter. Now, what do ye think?"

She smiled and handed him her outgoing mail.

"I think it is very exciting, Mr. Donnell. Thank you very much."

He handed her the regular mail, and she gathered it up with the box and walked quickly down the street to the office. A flush had spread to her cheeks, but perhaps she could blame it on the warm morning rather than the mysterious box addressed to her in the hand of Étienne LeClair.

She had ten minutes to spare before opening time. Letitia locked the door behind her and set the box on her desk. It was very light, and she shook it, but it gave only the tiniest rustle. With a trembling hand, she took scissors from her drawer and cut the string that bound the parcel. Then she carefully removed the brown paper.

She lifted the lid and found two folded sheets of writing paper on top of crumpled newsprint. She opened the letter and read:

Dear Letitia,

Mr. Hunter has asked me to prepare a parcel for him in celebration of his daughter's birthday, which he regrets missing. He is hopeful this will reach you on the auspicious day or soon thereafter. Your father has been very busy inspecting the camps, making sure they are ready for the season ahead. He is also checking to see if they have the supplies of food and animal fodder spoken for and if the equipment is in working order. We were longer than expected at Spruce Run and the new camp above it, as Mr. Hunter wanted to see completion of the chimney and walls before he left.

Letitia plopped down in her chair, breathing raggedly, and read on.

He asked me to purchase something suitable for the occasion when I went to Quebec a few days ago, as there is no place on the Maine side of the border with merchandise to please a lovely young lady.

She wondered if Étienne were quoting her father, or if those were his own words.

So, you see, if this does not please you, it is not your father's fault. The guilt is mine, and I beg your indulgence. The towns I passed through were very small and the choices limited. However, I thought this might be acceptable. The old woman who made it is very skilled, having learned her craft from her grandmother, who came from Chantilly.

Unable to stand the suspense any longer, Letitia parted the layers of newspaper and drew out a delicate table runner of intricate lace. She gasped and took it to the window, holding it up to the light. Never had she seen such fine work. She went back to the desk and picked the letter up again.

It is my hope that this token will brighten your home and you will remember your father's love for you each time you view it.

Letitia knew it was not her father she would be thinking of when she saw the lovely lace gift. It was the man who had chosen it for her, who had sensed that she craved beauty and femininity.

There was more to the letter, and eagerly she read on.

I was able to visit my old home and was glad for the chance to see my family once more.

You asked me a question, and I would like to answer it now. I came to know Christ three years ago, at one of your father's lumber camps, the one at Flood Pond. Every year a preacher comes to the camps in winter and preaches God's Word to the men. Some of them, or us, I should say, listen, and some do not. That year, I listened. It was with great wonder that I realized I was a sinner in need of redemption. I will always be grateful to Mr. Hunter for allowing the missionary to visit the camps. My mother is also a believer in Christ, and one of my brothers, but I continue to pray for the rest. Perhaps you would join me in this prayer.

She bowed her head at once, breathing out both gratitude and supplication. The privilege of praying for Étienne's family warmed her with an inner joy. And Étienne had rejoined her father! He would be back in a couple of weeks. Her prayers had been answered, and their friendship was no longer tentative, but solid, and she knew it would last. If this was to be the extent of it, she would be satisfied.

Her stomach fluttered as she turned to the second sheet. At the bottom was a tiny but lifelike drawing of a man cowering in the branches of a spindly tree, while a moose snorted menacingly below. She plunged eagerly into the letter once more.

Your father and I will move on in the morning to French Joe Camp, but I will entrust this package to a man going south, and I will pray that it reaches you safely. The men have had encounters in this area with l'original, as we call the moose. It is my hope that the messenger will not be chased up a tree and left clutching your birthday gift as l'original paws angrily below.

And now, Miss Letitia, if you do not mind, I would like to
wish you a happy birthday, and it is with anticipation that I
consider our return.

Sincerely,
Étienne

There was a knock at the door, and Letitia jumped, realizing it was well after eight o'clock. She should have opened the office. She thrust the letter into her desk drawer and hurried to open the door. John Rawley stood on the stoop.

"Ah, Miss Hunter."

Letitia shrank back, hoping her serviceable work clothes were plain enough to snuff any admiration he might otherwise feel for her.

"Mr. Rawley," she said evenly. "My father is touring his lumber camps. May I help you this morning?"

"Yes, I wanted to see if my lumber has been sawn yet. Your father promised last spring that it would be dry when I needed it."

"We have the native spruce in the drying sheds," Letitia said, moving back into the office. "The other woods are being brought in. If you would like to speak to our mill supervisor, Raymond Linden, I'm sure he can give the exact status of each component of the order."

Rawley eyed her with mild surprise. "And when do you expect Mr. Hunter to be back?"

"Not for at least two weeks," she replied. "If there is anything you wish to communicate to him, I will be writing to him today."

"No, no, that's fine," Rawley said. "I'll step over to the mill and see Linden." He walked toward the door, and Letitia reflected that the handsome man, with his broad shoulders and luxuriant mustache, still held no appeal for her. He swung around at the door, with his hand on the knob, and appraised her again.

"I would offer you lunch, Miss Hunter, but I suspect you

would turn me down flat."

Flatter than a pancake, she thought. "I try to stay near the office these days, but I thank you for your kind invitation." She smiled cordially.

He nodded, his eyes thoughtful, then went out and shut the door.

Letitia turned her attention back to her package and folded the lace carefully. When she was ready to place it back inside the flat rectangular box, she noticed another sheet of paper in the bottom and lifted it out.

> *Dear Letitia,*
> *My heartiest wishes for a happy birthday. I regret I was not there to celebrate with you.*
>
> > *Your fond father*

She smiled. So he hadn't left the entire process to his assistant, after all.

&

Letitia went about her duties that day with a light heart and allowed herself three times to take out Étienne's letter and read it over. By the end of the day, she knew its contents by heart and savored its nuances. She had not offended him with her letter, and, most telling of all, he was looking forward to his return.

She decided to send one more missive to her father, and also one to Étienne. Their final stop before coming home would be a farm on the edge of the northern forest, where a middle-aged farmer raised Belgian horses. Lincoln Hunter bought horses from him each year for the lumber operations. His loggers used the massive animals to haul logs out of the forest on the smooth snow to the river.

> *Dear Father,*
> *Thank you so much for your birthday greetings and the*

*lovely gift. It was with great surprise that I opened the
package and discovered the beautiful lace runner. I have never
seen anything of such fine workmanship. It is incredible to
me that I have reached the advanced age of one and twenty,
but here I am. All is well at the office. Mr. Rawley was here
today, and I sent him to Mr. Linden for a report on his order.
I look forward to your return.*

*Your loving daughter,
Letitia*

That out of the way, she settled down to the demanding but
more pleasant task of framing her reply to Étienne. Her heart
hammered as she carefully penned:

Dear Étienne,
    *It is my hope that this letter will reach you at Turnbridge
Farm and that you and my father are in good health. The box
indeed arrived, so you see, the messenger had no untoward
encounters with l'original or other menacing creatures.
My father's birthday gift is lovely, and I appreciate the
thoughtfulness with which it was chosen. I tremendously
enjoyed your drawing. I hope you have not been among those
who have faced an angry moose.*
    *I do not think you have been able to attend services on your
journey north, and I think of you each time I go to church. I
pray that our heavenly Father will bless you from His Word
and that you will have fellowship with other believers.*

I sound like a schoolmarm, she admonished herself. She strove
for a more friendly touch, without sliding too far into intimacy.

    *I also pray for you and your family each day, and I accept
your birthday greeting with pleasure. I'm glad you were able
to make the journey to your family home.*
    If you are able to wire me from Bangor, it would please me

*to meet you and Father at the station when you return. I look
forward to having you both back here. The office seems very
empty these days.*

Sincerely,
Letitia

She reread the text and paused, uncertain whether to let the
letter leave her hands or not. When Étienne returned, she was
sure they would be more than coworkers. She rejoiced in that,
and mailed the letter.

❧

The next morning she was startled when John Rawley appeared
once again at the office.

"Miss Hunter, I have some concerns about the lumber for
the courthouse. Since your father is not available, may I discuss
it with you?"

Apprehension settled over Letitia. She swallowed and
dredged up all the courage and confidence she could find
deep within her. "Of course. Won't you sit down?"

Rawley pulled a chair over and sat facing her. "I spoke with
Linden yesterday."

"Yes. Is there a problem?"

"For starters, I'm concerned that the lumber is not all in
hand yet."

"Father has ordered everything you requested. We have
approximately half your requirement in the drying sheds, I
believe, and the rest will be shipped all sawn or will come here
as logs to be sawn within a month. When you need your finish
lumber in the spring, it will be delivered in good time."

"It must be fully dried."

"I'm sure it will be." She kept pasted on her face what she
hoped was a confident smile.

"Perhaps we should discuss other options." Rawley looked
sharply into her eyes.

"Other options?" Letitia barely escaped stuttering. If she

botched the order for her father's largest client in his absence, the fur would fly when he returned. "Would you please explain yourself, sir?"

"I need to be sure that lumber will be ready, and dry, when I need it."

"But you don't need it until next spring."

"April first."

"I see no problem in Northern Lumber delivering it by then."

He stared at her, and she felt uneasy. She knew he had discussed the delivery date with her father the day he placed the order.

"Perhaps you would have lunch with me a week from today and apprise me of the situation," he said. "If the operation is on schedule, I'll feel much better."

"I will send a report around to your office that day," she countered.

"No, I need the assurance only the owner can give me, in person."

"The owner, as you know, is still out on business."

"But you represent him."

"Yes."

"Then I would like to make an appointment. At noon next Friday, at the Maplewood. I will meet you there promptly at twelve, and you will have the facts ready," Rawley said firmly as he rose.

Letitia cast about in her mind for a retort that would put him in his place without jeopardizing his business with her father but could think of none. A flush crept into her cheeks as Rawley strode to the door. She couldn't just let him walk out. *Father, this is not right!* she prayed silently. *Make me wise.* She jumped to her feet.

"You would not speak so to my father," she called after him, and he stopped in the open doorway.

"Perhaps you are right. Your father is not a pretty girl who holds men at arm's length. He is a rational man who knows business. If you are going to represent him, you must learn to think like a man."

He went out the door.

Letitia was furious. She stood shaking for a moment, then sank into her chair. She certainly was not a man, but that did not mean she was irrational. Was Rawley sneering at her or pursuing her? Perhaps they were the same for him.

One thing Letitia knew: She would not have lunch with John Rawley the following Friday.

૨ન

Over the weekend, Letitia pondered Rawley's visits to the office. She had known he was attracted to her. Perhaps he was trying to press the issue in her father's absence and her recalcitrance had pushed him to speak in anger.

She prayed a great deal and took solace in the church services on Sunday. Her battered spirit found rest and peace in worship. She would survive this test by relying on God.

If Rawley withdrew his order in retaliation for her coldness, she would stand before Lincoln Hunter on his return and tell him exactly what had happened. She was sure he wouldn't like it, but she thought he would take her side. This clash with Rawley would never have happened had her father been home. And she wished Étienne were there. She felt somehow that his piercing brown eyes would cut through Rawley's pretense and unmask his true motives.

The more she thought about it, the more she was certain she had heard a threat in the contractor's words. Was the proposed luncheon an ultimatum, with loss of the contract the consequence of defying him?

She worked hard all week, keeping close tabs on the mill's production. The smaller orders were filled, and oak logs came in. Linden turned once more to sawing Rawley's required boards. They were a week into September, and the nights were chilly. In a few more weeks the lumberjacks would return to the camps and begin the winter's harvest.

Letitia did not confide in Linden about Rawley's visit, but the supervisor became edgy whenever she walked over to the mill. She realized she was checking on him two or three times a day, which would make any employee nervous.

On Thursday, she tried to stay out of the mill. Linden was competent and had assured her several times he would move the job along as fast as could be done safely. She worked over her accounts and dealt with clients. Two young Frenchmen came to inquire about work, and she sent them to Jacques to see if he needed more hands in the lumberyard. She realized she was fretting, partly over Rawley and partly because she had had no word from the travelers for a week.

Late in the afternoon, Linden came into the office.

"Miss Hunter, I thought you would be over to see how we're doing," he said with a strained smile.

"No, Mr. Linden. I know you're doing a good job, and I decided not to hound you about it."

He smiled. "Well, thank you. Things are going forward."

"The Rawley order is on schedule, then?"

"Yes, or a little ahead of what we expected."

"So I can send word to the client that all is well?"

"Yes, if you think that is necessary." Linden looked keenly at her.

Letitia returned the look. Her father trusted Linden, she knew. He had been with Northern Lumber for more than twenty years, and mill supervisor for ten.

"Miss Hunter," he ventured, "is there a problem with the Rawley order?"

"I...don't think so," she faltered.

"You seem anxious about it."

She looked down at the open ledger on her desk. "Well, Mr. Rawley seems anxious about it."

"Did he complain to you last week after he came to the mill? I showed him what we've done and assured him we would have the lumber in plenty of time, to his specifications."

"He expressed concern about the lumber being dry in time."

Linden nodded. "I went over the timetable with him. There's nothing to worry about. It's fine."

Letitia frowned. "Then why did he——?" She broke off. Rawley had come to her the next day and intimidated her, implying that things were not moving along as they should. It occurred to her that perhaps she should call on Mr. Warren, her father's lawyer.

"Is everything all right, Miss Hunter?" Linden asked.

"Other than Mr. Rawley, everything's fine," she assured him. "And Father ought to be home in another week, two at the most."

He nodded. "I expect the last of the red oak to come in soon. We'll saw it out when it arrives."

Letitia sat at her desk after he had gone. She wished she had a way to reach her father, but she couldn't be sure where he was now. Maybe at Turnbridge Farm, maybe still at one of the lumber camps. She might send a wire to the farm, but she didn't know if it would be delivered. Turnbridge was a good twenty miles beyond Bangor. Her father wouldn't want her to send for him unless it was an emergency.

Should she go to Mr. Warren? She balked at that. Mark Warren would make a fuss and probe into the matter and embarrass her. This wasn't a legal matter. It was a business matter, between her and Rawley. Or was it a personal matter?

She sighed and closed the office for the night.

fourteen

On Friday morning, Letitia paced nervously across the office to Étienne's desk, then turned and walked back to her own. Noon at the Maplewood. She wouldn't do it.

At ten o'clock, she went to the lumberyard and asked Jacques for a man to run an errand for her. He gave her a twelve-year-old boy whom he had employed short-term to help stack the boards for the large Rawley order.

"What is your name?" Letitia asked as they walked toward the office together.

"Pierre Levesque, *ma'm'selle.*"

"Pierre, I need for you to take a message to a gentleman for me. Come into the office and I will give you the message."

At her desk, she picked up the report Linden had sent over from the mill half an hour earlier. It stated that all of the spruce lumber for Rawley's order was sawn and drying nicely and that three-fourths of the red oak was sawn. The rest was in production.

On a sheet of paper she wrote:

Dear Sir,

From this report by my mill supervisor, you can see that your order is in good hands. Things are progressing nicely, and I am sure the service afforded by Northern Lumber will please you. I see no need for us to meet to discuss the matter.

Sincerely,
L. Hunter

"There now." She entrusted the note and the report into Pierre's hands. "Here is the address. If you deliver this to Mr.

Rawley personally, I shall give you a bonus."

"Oui, ma'm'selle." His dark eyes glittered. *"J'attendrai la réponse?"*

Letitia considered. Should she have him wait for an answer? "If he tells you to wait, then do it; but if he says nothing, just come back and report to me."

He sped out the door, and Letitia couldn't help but smile at his eagerness. She began writing a letter to a supplier of exotic woods and tried to forget about Rawley.

Fifteen minutes later, he marched into her office, slamming the door in the face of the French boy, who was panting at his heels.

"Miss Hunter, what is the meaning of this?" He held up her note.

Letitia took a deep breath and stood. "The meaning is good news, sir. Your lumber is going to be just as you ordered it. I'm confident it will be premium dry lumber. End of discussion."

"End of nothing," he roared. "We have an appointment in exactly"—he pulled out his pocket watch—"one hour."

Letitia tried to speak soothingly, although she was trembling. "Sir, I see no need for that. There is nothing to discuss."

"Nothing except your pride!" he shouted.

Letitia took an involuntary step back.

"You have rebuffed me time and again." Rawley's face reddened and his eyes snapped with anger.

"I—"

Letitia cringed as he roared, "I demand to know what you have against me! You surely cannot think I'm not good enough—"

The street door swung open with a crash, and Letitia jumped. Étienne filled the doorway, looking first at her, then at the raging contractor.

Rawley rounded on LeClair. "Get out!" he shouted. "I am speaking with Miss Hunter!"

Letitia's heart pounded. What was he doing here? And was her father on his way as well?

Étienne held up his hands, palms outward. "Be calm, *m'sieur.*

Mademoiselle does not wish you to shout, I believe."

Letitia's shock at seeing him gave way to pride and gratitude for her champion.

Rawley glared at Étienne. "This is a private conversation!"

"*Non*, m'sieur, *pardonnez-moi*, but this is not the conversation. It is what we call the shouting match. I will not permit you to abuse Miss Hunter."

Letitia's empathy swelled when she heard Étienne's lapse in grammar. She knew his English was flawless except when he was agitated.

She stepped forward. "Mr. LeClair is right, Mr. Rawley. I do not put up with shouting in my office. No *man* would, either. If you wish to discuss business, please sit down and speak calmly, but I contend there is nothing to discuss."

He stood facing her for a moment, his lips twitching slightly.

"If I prefer to not continue doing business with Northern Lumber, then what?"

Letitia hoped her dismay did not show on her face. "Then I will tell my father that the order is withdrawn, sir." Unable to stand any longer because her knees were wobbly, she sat down, hoping it looked intentional.

"Sir, you cannot do this," Étienne said.

Rawley whirled toward him. "Who says I can't?"

"Does not m'sieur have a contract? Mr. Hunter's advocate will say this."

Letitia regretted not going to Mark Warren, after all. She said shakily, "Yes, that's right, Mr. LeClair. Mr. Warren will discuss the matter with Mr. Rawley, I'm sure. I can send the boy around to ask him to see Mr. Rawley today." She glanced toward the doorway, but the boy had disappeared.

Rawley stepped closer to her desk and stood looking down at her. For five seconds he neither moved nor spoke. Étienne stayed solidly in the doorway. Letitia tried to return Rawley's stare without flinching.

"*Pardon!* Everything is all right?" said a deep voice, and

Letitia darted a glance toward the doorway. Jacques Laplante loomed on the doorstep, addressing Étienne. The boy peeked around his elbow.

"Everything is fine," Étienne said. "Miss Hunter is having a discussion with a client."

Rawley cleared his throat. "Forgive me, Miss Hunter. I am not accustomed to losing my temper with ladies."

She returned his gaze. "And I am not accustomed to being browbeaten by our clients."

He sighed. "Please accept my apology. The lumber order stands. It is fine, I'm sure. Your father is a shrewd man. It. . . surprised me that he left his business in the hands of a novice."

Letitia said quietly, "I am competent, sir. I don't see why you should wish to punish my father because of your dislike of me. However, if you wish to discuss transferring your order to another firm with my attorney. . ."

"No," Rawley said firmly. "That would set me back months. It wasn't my intention to renege on the agreement."

"Then what was your intention?" she asked, surprised at her own boldness.

He hesitated, then glanced toward Étienne and Jacques still towering in the doorway. "Could I have a word with you alone, Miss Hunter?"

Spending another moment alone with John Rawley was the last thing she wanted, but she didn't want to humiliate him before the men and Pierre when he seemed ready to reason. She looked toward them. "Mr. LeClair, if you and Mr. Laplante would be kind enough to wait outside, I will call you if I need you."

"*Certainement*, mademoiselle," said Étienne. He went out, and Jacques pushed Pierre gently before them. The door closed, but Letitia was confident her protectors were only inches from the door.

"What is it you wish to say?"

He sat down, his face set in contrition. "I did not set out to alienate you and disrupt our business agreement. Quite the contrary, I. . .was hoping for an opportunity to further our acquaintance."

Letitia swallowed and tried to quell the distaste that filled her heart. "Mr. Rawley, I will be frank. I have no desire to further a personal acquaintance with a man with such a temper as I have seen displayed here today."

"I understand. Please believe me, I regret this scene, and if you change your mind—"

"I won't change my mind. Sir, you have called me a novice and implied that I am too feminine in my thinking, whatever that means. These are insults, and it seems a strange way to attract a woman, if that was indeed your design."

He sat silent a moment. "I cannot fault what you say. I will take my leave, Miss Hunter, and perhaps we would best forget this exchange. I will not bother you again about the lumber but will do business with your father when he returns."

She sighed with relief when he left. Étienne, Jacques, and Pierre came into the office.

"Mademoiselle is all right?" Jacques eyed her anxiously.

"Yes, thank you. But, Étienne, where is my father? I didn't expect to see you here—and without him. What has happened?"

The lines of his face went flat and grave. She noticed as he came toward her that he had not shaved that morning, and dark stubble shadowed his face.

When he reached her side, he startled her by dropping to one knee beside her chair and reaching for her hand.

"Letitia, it grieves me to tell you this, but apparently I have outdistanced the telegram I sent you from Bangor. You did not receive my message?"

She stared at him in confusion. His gentle touch thrilled her, but his words and his troubled demeanor frightened her.

"What is it?" she gasped. "Please tell me."

"Your father is ill." He paused, gazing into her eyes as though to gauge her distress. "He is still at Turnbridge Farm. I left him there at dawn and rode as fast as I could to the train station. I sent a telegram, and I hoped it would reach you before I did, but apparently it has miscarried."

Letitia felt her lips tremble, and she put her fingers up to still them. "How bad is it?"

"We had the doctor come yesterday, and he did not like what he saw. He came again early this morning, and he advised me to fetch you. That is why I am here, mon amie. I will take you to him. Come, we will go first to your house so that you can pack whatever you need."

"Oh, yes. Thank you."

"We have an empty wagon in the lumberyard, all hitched up," Jacques said. "Take that."

"Thank you, I will," said Étienne.

Letitia stood and glanced uncertainly around the room. "Should I just close the office?"

Étienne's brow furrowed. "You may be gone several days, I fear. Perhaps while you are packing, I can step around to Mr. Weston's house and see if he would be willing to come in and keep things going during this crisis."

"Yes, thank you." She noticed Pierre then. The boy stood near the door, his lips twitching. "*Mille mercis*, Pierre."

"I met him at the corner as I came from the station," Étienne said. "He begged me to help you. He said the rich gentleman was yelling at mademoiselle."

"And he ran into the yard a few moments ago," Jacques added. "He told me to come quick; mademoiselle needed me."

She smiled. "I promised Pierre a bonus for delivering my message to Mr. Rawley, but he deserves far more for fetching the two of you."

She opened her desk drawer and took out the two one-dollar bills left from the five dollars her father had given her nearly a month earlier.

"Voilà, Pierre," she said, holding the two dollars out to the boy. His eyes grew round, and he looked up at her with distress on his face.

"Non, non, ma'm'selle! C'est de *trop!*"

"It *is* too much," Jacques agreed.

"Far from it," Letitia replied. "Pierre, you must keep the money, young man. You have earned it."

Pierre turned his huge brown eyes on Jacques, and the big man laughed. "Keep it."

The boy smiled in adoration at Letitia. "Merci, ma'm'selle."

He dashed out the door.

"Come, now," Étienne said with a gentle smile. "I will escort you home, then go and see Mr. Weston. If he cannot help us, I will see if Mr. Linden has a trustworthy man who can keep the office open for a few days. I need to inform him of your father's illness anyway."

"I can tell Linden," Jacques said. "And I am very sorry about your father, mademoiselle." He left the office with a sympathetic smile.

Letitia stood and straightened her desk, then walked to the coat tree where her bonnet hung. As she reached for it, the door opened, and a strange boy entered the office.

"Telegram for Miss Lettie Hunter."

Letitia grimaced at his pronunciation of her name and held out her hand. "Thank you." She looked toward her desk but realized she'd given Pierre the last of her cash.

Étienne reached in his pocket and handed the boy a coin.

"My message, no doubt," he said as the boy left.

Letitia nodded, but she opened it anyway.

> *LH very ill. I will arrive Zimmerville 11 a.m. and bring you to him.*
>
> *E. LeClair*

As she stared at the bleak words, tears welled in her eyes, and the gravity of the situation hit her with the force of a hurricane. Her father's condition must be severe indeed for Étienne to leave his side to get her.

He touched her elbow lightly. "Come, *ma belle*. I will take you home."

A sob shook her, and she felt her courage splintering. Étienne wrapped her in his strong arms and held her against his chest. She crumpled the telegram in her hand and leaned against him. His warmth comforted her, and for a moment she wished she could stay forever in his embrace and not face the sorrow that surely awaited her at Turnbridge Farm.

Slowly she slid her arms around him, and he stroked her back. His cheek came down gently against her hair, putting a warm pressure on her head, and she closed her eyes.

"Letitia," he whispered, "I will do everything in my power to help you. We must hurry, though, *ma chérie*. We will take the 1:35 train."

"Can we make it?"

"I think so. Come."

fifteen

An hour later, Étienne knocked on the door of the Hunter mansion. Mrs. Watkins opened it, her face pinched and pale.

"Come in!" she cried. "Tell me about the master. Miss Letitia says he's very ill and you're carrying her off to the north lands."

"Yes, it is true. We have not much time to reach the station. Jacques Laplante has brought the wagon to carry our bags, and we must hurry."

Letitia came down the stairs carrying a satchel, and he stepped forward. His heart wrenched at the sight of her bloodshot eyes. But she had changed into a dove gray dress and bonnet and held her back straight.

"I'm ready," she said.

"Come, then." He took her bag and offered his arm.

"Mrs. Watkins, thank you for agreeing to stay here," Letitia said.

"Oh, that's nothing. Don't you worry about the house. Everything will be fine."

Étienne escorted Letitia down the wide steps. Jacques leaped forward and took her luggage while Étienne assisted her onto the wagon seat.

On the short ride to the station, Jacques reached over and squeezed Letitia's hand.

"Angelique and I, we will pray for you and the boss."

"Thank you." Letitia turned to Étienne, who sat on the other side of her. "Did you see Mr. Weston?"

"Yes. He will go in this afternoon. And Mr. Linden said he would send Marston, one of his foremen, if needed. He's not trained in accounting, but he can deal with clients who come in. Between him and Mr. Weston, all should be well."

"Thank you so much," Letitia said with a sigh. Her eyes clouded with anxiety. "Oh, the payroll! I left the account and payroll ledgers in my desk."

"Do not worry," Étienne said gently. "Mr. Weston assured me he will handle the payroll and other financial accounts. Do not distress yourself, *mon amie*."

She settled against the seat. "You're right. Thank you."

He wished he could offer her more comfort, but under Jacques' sharp eye he didn't dare touch her. She had allowed him to hold her briefly at the office, and he sensed that she understood how deeply he cared about her. Being here beside her was the right thing for this moment.

"Do you expect to be gone long?" Jacques asked, looking at him past Letitia.

Étienne hesitated. "I do not know what we shall find at Turnbridge, but I will try to get word to you soon."

Jacques nodded and turned the team in at the depot.

❧

The train was boarding, and Jacques walked briskly with them to the platform and handed their luggage to the porter.

He took Letitia's hand. "*Bon voyage*, mademoiselle. Your papa will be happy to see such a pretty thing come to cheer him."

She gulped, hoping she could avoid weeping.

"He will mend," Jacques assured her.

"I don't know, Jacques. It sounds very serious." She shot a glance toward Étienne, who waited for her a pace away.

"Ah, well. Many will be praying."

"Thank you."

"Étienne will take good care of you, *mon enfant*."

"Yes, I think he will. *Au revoir*, Jacques. Merci, mon ami." She smiled at him a little shakily.

Étienne extended a hand to help her mount the steps of the passenger car. Even though she wore cotton gloves, his touch exhilarated her. The prospect of being alone with him on the train ride after being apart for a month unnerved her a little.

Their relationship had changed since he left with her father. His warm embrace at the office after he broke the news to her was proof of that. Her face colored as she remembered that moment, and she paused in the aisle.

"Sit here, mademoiselle, if it is to your liking," Étienne said softly from behind her.

She sank gratefully onto the seat and slid over near the window. Étienne placed his hat on the overhead rack and settled beside her with a mournful smile.

"What will happen when we reach Bangor?" she asked.

"I left Mr. Turnbridge's team at a stable in Bangor. He is very concerned for Mr. Hunter and has great respect for him. Yesterday he sent me for the best physician to be had."

"That is good to know." She realized that he'd had no time to rest during his brief return to Zimmerville.

"Did you have dinner?" she asked.

"Jacques gave me a sandwich from his dinner pail when he brought the wagon back. How about you?"

"I—yes—well, of sorts. You know Mrs. Watkins."

"Ah, yes. You were too nervous to eat, but she insisted."

She couldn't help but smile. "You are right." The train began to move. She inhaled sharply as her thoughts once more reverted to her father. "Étienne?" she whispered.

"What, mon amie?"

"What exactly is wrong with my father?"

His eyes filled with compassion, and he covered her gloved hand with his. "I am afraid it is very bad. He seemed fatigued all through the journey, once we left Bangor. I thought when I returned from Quebec that he looked more rested. But when we got to Nine Mile Camp, he was exhausted. We rested there, and he seemed better, but I think the horseback trip we made to the new camp took a lot out of him."

Letitia sucked in a breath. "It was hard traveling?"

"Yes. The road was in very poor shape. He was tired and dizzy the night we arrived at Round Pond. I urged him to stay an extra day, but he wanted to push on to Turnbridge Farm. By the time we arrived, late that afternoon, he could barely stand up." His eyes were troubled. "I apologize, Letitia. I should have insisted he wait at Round Pond. But your father. . .he is very. . ."

She smiled ruefully. "Yes, I understand. Father is the one who gives the orders."

"Exactly. I thought if he rested a few days. . ."

Letitia nodded.

"The next morning I could see that he was very ill, and I urged him to stay in bed. When he did not disagree, I knew it was bad." Étienne hung his head. "He. . .complained of a pain." His look of distress raised her apprehension. "Mr. Turnbridge told me where to get the doctor, and I went immediately. Letitia, I fear it is very serious. The doctor says it is his heart. That is why I made the decision to come for you."

"I'm glad you did." She squeezed his hand, and he sat looking down at their clasped fingers.

"When I left this morning, he seemed a little easier. The doctor could not stay, but he promised to call again later today. There may be some word when we reach Bangor."

"And how long will it take us to reach the farm?"

"Several hours, depending on the roads and the horses, but Turnbridge's teams are fast. Perhaps three or four hours."

She nodded, meeting his gaze soberly. "I'm glad you are with me, Étienne."

"Oh, ma chérie, if I could—" He broke off and stared forward, his mouth in a grim line.

Her heart fluttered at his endearment and also at his evident distress. "Do not blame yourself," she said.

He sighed deeply and settled back against the seat cushion but kept her hand clasped in his.

After a few minutes, the conductor came down the aisle, and Étienne released her hand to reach into his pocket for their tickets. She had noticed his new suit earlier, but she observed him closely while the conductor distracted him. The suit was well cut but not tailor-made. She wondered if her father had a hand in the increase of his wardrobe. Or was Étienne using money he would rather send home to his mother in order to dress in a manner that would please his boss?

She untied her bonnet and removed it. When the conductor moved away, Étienne asked, "May I take that for you, mademoiselle?"

"Yes, thank you."

While he stored her bonnet above and opened the side window, she removed her white gloves. It was a warm day for mid-September, and the air in the car was nearly stifling. Étienne dropped the window sash, and a cool breeze flowed in and ruffled her hair.

"Too much?" he asked.

"No, it's heavenly."

He smiled and settled back beside her.

Letitia folded her hands in her lap and wondered what the proper etiquette was for traveling with a man. She had made a few trips with her father, but this was different. Should she try to keep the conversation going, and if so, what topics were deemed suitable?

She darted a glance toward him and found his warm brown eyes were resting on her. She caught her breath and looked away. The rhythm of the wheels quickened as the train left the city.

"Letitia." He had leaned close to be heard above the noise of the train.

She turned toward him and was startled at his nearness. "Y–yes?"

He drew back a little. "I am very sorry your father is ill, but it does not completely outweigh my delight in seeing you again." He watched her steadily, as though trying to gauge her response.

Letitia found it hard to breathe steadily. Yes, everything had changed. She had wanted this, but now that she faced the reality, she wasn't sure she was ready. She swallowed hard.

He glanced around, and she looked, too. There were perhaps

a dozen other passengers in the car, spread out over its length. None were immediately behind or in front of them, though there was a gentleman across the aisle.

"Your letters...," he said, leaning close.

She nodded.

"They gave me hope."

Again she nodded.

"Letitia..."

She looked up into his handsome, strong face. His kindness warmed her, but she also caught a touch of insecurity in his wrinkled brow. After his first uneasy day in Zimmerville last winter, he had given her the impression of quiet confidence as he adjusted to his new surroundings. Now he seemed once more slightly at sea.

"I—you—" She gave up and turned away, reddening.

"What is it?" he asked, near her ear.

She stared out the window. They were passing a lake edged with hardwoods, and the leaves were beginning to turn crimson and gold. She soaked up the beauty of the afternoon light on the trees and water.

She took a deep breath and turned away from the window and faced him. "I've prayed so hard that we could be friends. The Lord seems to have answered my prayers."

"Yes." It was almost a question.

Letitia felt she had said the wrong thing. Would he take it to mean she wanted only to be friends, nothing more?

He put his hand on hers. She slowly turned her palm upward and grasped his fingers. He glanced at the man across the aisle, who seemed oblivious. Étienne drew her hand through the crook of his arm and covered it with his warm fingers, stroking it and not looking at her. She sat very still, thinking, *I'll become accustomed to this. I will.*

They sat without speaking as the miles passed beneath them and lay in neat lines behind them. Her heart raced faster than the train. Gradually it slowed, and her stomach stopped churning. Only now and then a jolt of joy shot through her, even as concern for her father caused sorrow.

Étienne leaned toward her. "You could sleep, perhaps."

"No," she replied. "I certainly could not."

He squeezed her hand and sat back beside her as the miles passed by.

๖

They reached Bangor just after four o'clock, and Étienne claimed their luggage.

"Are you sure you don't want to rest here until morning?" he asked, stooping a little to look down into her blue eyes beneath the brim of her bonnet.

"No, I'd rather get on to Father. That is, if you're not too tired."

"I am ready to go if you are certain," he replied.

"I am."

"Come, then. We must go to the stable."

Étienne found a hack just outside the depot and instructed the driver to take them to the livery stable. The sprawling city of Bangor still made him a little nervous, but he was beginning to feel comfortable getting back and forth from the station to the stable. He was sure he would get lost if he ever had to venture off that short route.

She smiled at him, a timid but hopeful smile that told him she was still as uncertain as he what the future held for them. The rattle of wheels and the clop of horses' hooves camouflaged the beating of his heart.

When they reached the stable, he helped harness the horses to Turnbridge's farm wagon and placed their luggage in the wagon bed. He helped Letitia onto the seat and climbed up beside her, taking the reins from the ostler.

It took all his concentration to guide the team until they struck the road that would take them north, away from the hubbub of the city and into the quiet countryside. The horses fell into a brisk trot, and he sighed and settled against the board seat's back. After several minutes' consideration, he shifted all the reins into his left hand and reached for Letitia's hand once more. She glanced up at him, a smile on her lips.

"If I do not offend you," he murmured.

"You do not."

He nodded, and they sat in silence for a few precious minutes, while he regained control of his heart, which was doing cartwheels and backflips a circus performer would envy.

"I suppose it will get dark before we are there," Letitia said.

"Yes, I fear you are right. But we have a lantern in the back, and some traveling robes if you get cold."

"The road is not bad so far," she said.

"No, it is good near the city. But the farther out we get, the worse the ruts. Still, it is not so bad this time of year as it will be next spring."

He watched her face as new scenery spread before them: fields of dry cornstalks, bathed in late afternoon sunlight; orchards heavy with fruit; and a large stand of scarlet sugar maples, with a little cabin nestled among the old trees. She seemed to take delight in every new vista. At last they entered the forest, and he could barely make out the road ahead in the shadows. But the team knew the way home and went rapidly along.

"So, three or four hours?" she asked timidly.

"If we could keep up this pace, we'd be there in two hours more," he said. "But I came over this road yesterday, and I know it gets worse."

The wind increased, and Letitia shivered. Étienne reached behind him and pulled a lap robe from the wagon box.

"Put this over your knees, chérie."

He had not meant to let the sweet name leave his lips again, but when he glanced at her face, she did not seem displeased.

"You must be chilly, too," she said.

His linen jacket was not as warm as the woolen one he had put away in Waterville. He considered stopping to open his bag and take out the black jacket.

"Perhaps you could share a corner of the robe," Letitia said softly.

She moved closer to him in the twilight, and he pulled the edge of the lap robe over his knees. He drove on, very happy. He longed to take her hand in his again, but he must preserve propriety at all costs. After all, it was getting dark, and she was a lady, and one in a sorrowful situation at that. This was not really a proper time for courting, even if he had her father's consent, which he did not. He decided he would do better to give his attention to the horses.

Soon the big Belgians slowed to a walk, and Étienne barely guided them, letting them choose their own path in the roadway.

"Sleep if you can," he said.

"I can't. I keep thinking about Father."

"He is in my prayers constantly," Étienne said.

"Mine, too. Thank you for praying for him. It is my wish that God will spare him. But if not, what then, Étienne?" In the dimness, he could not read her expression, but her voice told him much about her sorrow. "I can't bring myself to think what I would do if Father were incapacitated or—or worse."

"If that time should come, the Lord will guide you." As he said it, he realized he believed every word. "Your father has friends who would be competent to advise you. And this month you have proven yourself able to run the business."

"Oh, but that was only temporary until Father and—you—returned."

"I am but a cog in the wheel," he said. "A very small, insignificant, replaceable cog."

"Don't say that. My father has come to depend on you."

"Well, I don't say he hasn't, but we have been beyond civilization. When we return to Zimmerville, he may forget the things he said to me in the north woods."

She was quiet for a moment then asked, "What sort of things did he say to you?"

"He mentioned a trip he planned to make to Philadelphia

after Christmas. He...said he might send me in his place."

"But, Étienne! That's wonderful. It means he trusts you as Northern Lumber's official representative."

"Well, I don't know. He did not say for sure that he would do that. It was only a possibility, if. . ."

"If what?"

"If I do well between now and then. He said he would educate me further and see that I had time to study accounting and economics. He mentioned several times sending me out on business for him. He said—" He stopped abruptly. Some of the things the boss had said in his moments of pain were not meant for Letitia's ears.

"What?" she asked softly.

"I do not wish to distress you."

Immediately he heard alarm in her voice. "What is it, Étienne?"

He sighed and flicked the reins to keep the horses at a trot. "Your father said he is getting too old to travel. When he first became ill, he complained a bit. Not much, you understand."

"Oh, I understand." Letitia smiled. "You should have seen him two winters ago, when he had influenza. I know what a difficult patient he can be."

"Well, he said that he ought to quit traipsing about in the winter and send a younger man to tour the camps and be sure all was well."

"Meaning you."

"So I understood. And then he began talking of me going to Philadelphia."

"My father does not speak rashly of things he doesn't mean to follow through on."

Étienne fell silent, thinking about the things Mr. Hunter had said to him in private. The horses pulled steadily on, snorting now and then.

"Letitia?" he began cautiously, eyeing her in the deepening darkness.

"Yes?"

He drove on for a minute, wondering whether it was wise to speak again. "I wanted to write to you and share my hope that your father would. . .permit me to. . .be a friend to his daughter."

"Did he give you reason to think so?" she asked. "That would be good news, indeed."

He laid his hand once more over hers and squeezed it.

"You are cold," she whispered. "You should have gloves."

He shifted the reins to his left hand, and she lifted the edge of the robe. He allowed her to pull his hand beneath it, and they sat with fingers clasped between them, beneath the thick covering. Slowly his hand began to warm. He knew that after a few minutes he would have to switch hands again, although it would mean relinquishing the sweet contact.

He thought back to his early days in the Northern Lumber Company office. She had sat all day, so prim and proper, not speaking to him; he'd known she was conscious of her father, yards away behind his massive walnut desk. Étienne had kept diligently to his paperwork, longing to speak to the beautiful Miss Hunter, or even just to glance at her now and then, but fearful of upsetting the stern owner.

"My father can be intimidating," she said.

He laughed. "You minimize the effect of his presence."

"Yes, perhaps that is so."

"He seemed to be. . .arranging suitors for you, or trying to. But you—you kept them all at a distance."

"The men he brought around did not seem right for me."

"I was glad," he admitted. "When you put Mr. Rawley aside, I was very glad. He would not have been a good match for you."

"Oh, yes, John Rawley," she said with distaste.

"Can you tell me why he was at the office today?"

She frowned. "May I tell you everything?"

"But yes."

She smiled, and he realized he'd lapsed in his syntax again. If he truly wanted to please her father, he would have to stop letting his French roots show through his speech.

"You'd better warm your other hand."

He squeezed her fingers and took his right hand out to hold the reins, shoving his left hand into the pocket of his jacket on the other side.

The horses came out into an open stretch, and the moon shone down on them, striking golden highlights in Letitia's hair and gleaming off the harness buckles.

"It's so bright," she noted. "How can it be so cold?"

"It is the time of year. I think it will freeze tonight. We are far north of Zimmerville now. The frost comes earlier here."

He reached into the wagon bed and pulled up a woolen blanket.

"Wrap this around your shoulders."

She complied and settled again beside him, her shoulder almost touching his.

"Now, then, you were going to tell me something," he said.

Letitia sighed. "John Rawley insisted that I meet him for lunch today, to tell him how his order was coming along. I refused to go, but. . .Étienne, I was afraid he would cancel his order if I defied him. I sent Pierre Levesque with a message saying the lumber was well into production and that the meeting was unnecessary."

"You sent Pierre? Rawley must have loved that!"

"Yes, he came storming into my office and slammed the door in Pierre's face."

"And the boy saw me coming up the street and ran to fetch me, then got Jacques from the lumberyard."

"Yes. Pierre was quite heroic. I'll always be glad he was there." Letitia was silent a moment; then she turned toward him in the moonlight, her face lined in thought. "I couldn't decide why he had spoken to me so rudely. Was it because he disdains women who aspire to commerce, or because he—?" She pressed her lips together and looked forward, toward the horses.

Étienne tried to reach beyond her words and catch her thoughts. "Yes, that was it, ma chérie."

sixteen

Letitia whirled and peered at him. "How do you know what I was going to say?"

"What *were* you going to say?"

"Well, I—" She paused once more, and he smiled.

"Your modesty will not let you say that he was angry because you showed no interest in him. I'm glad you refused to meet him."

"Yes," she admitted. "And I'm glad you came when you did, although the reason for your arrival saddens me. But if you had been there all along, perhaps Rawley would not have spoken as he did."

"Perhaps not."

She looked up into his eyes. "Why do you suppose he did that, when Father was away? He must have known the lumber would be good and that it would be ready on time. Do you suppose he mistrusts women that much?"

"No, I don't think he doubted your competence. And he knew you were only your father's proxy."

"Why then?"

"It is as we said. He has been attracted to you for months. Perhaps he thought he could break through your reserve when Mr. Hunter was out of the way."

"Perhaps. He was so angry."

"He had been denied the object of his ambition."

"Ambition? I would hardly call myself an object of ambition."

"Why not? You are a wealthy young woman."

She laughed. "I haven't a penny to my name. My father doesn't pay me for my labor. I had to go to the bank this afternoon for money for this trip."

"But, you see, you could do that. You could walk into the bank and ask for cash, and they would give it to you without question."

"Well, yes, because my father has authorized me. . ."

"Exactly, and you are his only daughter. Letitia, you are his heir."

She sat still. "You don't think—"

"Oh, don't I?"

"But. . .Étienne—"

"This is why young men like me must remain silent when they admire you."

"Because my father would think you—oh, no." Her upper lip quivered.

"Oh, yes, my dear Letitia! In your father's eyes, I am not a worthy man for you. He has said as much, has he not?"

She would not meet his gaze.

Étienne could not keep back a wry chuckle. "Perhaps I am foolish even now, thinking we can be friends. What is friendship when I desire so much more, and what hope have I of ever being suitable, so far as your father is concerned?"

Once more, she scrutinized his features in the moonlight, and his pulse raced. He longed to sweep her into his arms and kiss her, but what would that tell her, hard on the heels of their conversation about fortune hunters? She would think him no better than Rawley, who had tried to force himself on her.

"Perhaps I overstep the bounds even now," he said regretfully. "Letitia, I cannot speak. I have not the right."

They rode on over the rough road, and the silence between them lengthened. When his right hand was cold, he wanted to swap the reins to his left and reach for her warm, gloved hand beneath the robe again, but he didn't dare. He should not have set her thinking about men who aimed to marry for gain. She was pondering what he had said; he could tell. The chill deepened, and she pulled the blanket tight around her. Étienne drove on, deep in thought.

An hour later he said, "We will soon be there. I cannot tell you how much I have enjoyed being with you this night. Were it not for your father's need of you, I would not wish it to end."

Letitia smiled and said gently, "Nor would I."

His wayward pulse throbbed once more. It was no use. Even though he knew it was pointless, he could not deny his love for her.

The huge horses neighed and quickened their steps.

"We are close now," he explained. "They smell their home."

It was after eight o'clock when they trotted into the farmyard. Étienne stopped the team before the house and hopped down. Before he had tied them and helped Letitia down, the door opened and a white-haired man came out.

"LeClair?"

"Yes, sir, it's me."

"You brought Miss Hunter?"

"Yes, sir, here she is." He put his arms up to Letitia and swung her lightly to the ground.

"You must come in, young lady," the farmer said.

"How is my father?" she asked, stepping quickly forward.

"Not good. The doctor was here earlier and thought he was somewhat improved, but he's had a turn this evening."

Letitia walked quickly toward the lantern light spilling from the farmhouse's doorway.

"I'll put the horses away," Turnbridge said, going toward the team.

Étienne handed over the reins. "I thank you for the use of them."

"Well, your employer buys from me every year. I could not do less in his time of need."

Étienne followed Letitia into the kitchen of the farmhouse, where she removed her bonnet and coat.

"Let me take you to the room where your father is staying." He took a candle, lit it from the lantern on the kitchen table, and led her down a short hallway to the stairs.

At the top of the staircase, he turned to the left and showed her the door of a snug room. Another candle burned on a small table. The whitewashed wall sloped to meet the ceiling on one side, and a dormer window jutted from it. The room was dominated by a maple bed covered with several colorful, pieced quilts. Under them lay Mr. Hunter, very pale and thin.

Letitia gasped at the condition of her father. She stepped quickly to the bedside and lifted his hand. "Father!"

Étienne stood beside her. "He is sleeping now."

"He has lost weight," she said. "He looks gray."

"Yes," said Étienne. "He needs our prayers."

He pulled forward a chair with a padded tapestry seat. "Mr. Turnbridge must have been sitting with him. Do you wish to sit?"

"Yes, thank you." Letitia sank onto the chair, rubbing her father's hand.

He moaned, and his eyelids fluttered open. "Steve?" he called.

Étienne stepped close to the bedside and bent down so he would be within Lincoln Hunter's vision. "I am here, sir. May I help you?"

"My girl—"

"She's here, sir. I brought her." He stepped back, nodding at Letitia.

"Father! Father, I'm here with you now. You will be better soon, and I will take you home."

He squinted at her. "Letitia?"

"Yes, Father."

"You look like your mother."

She sat speechless, tears coursing down her cheeks.

Étienne drew a handkerchief from his pocket and handed it to her.

"Letitia, listen to me," her father said, struggling as if he would sit up.

"Take it easy, sir." Étienne placed his hand firmly on Lincoln's shoulder. "Just lie back and speak to your daughter. She will hear you."

The older man sank back on the feather pillow and lay breathing loudly. "Letitia, don't sell."

"I beg your pardon, Father?" she asked, her eyes widening.

"Don't sell the company."

"I—I won't, Father."

"Have to keep it in the family."

"Yes." She looked beseechingly up at Étienne, but he shrugged, feeling helpless.

"Northern Lumber will support you all your life if you're careful."

"Certainly, Father."

Lincoln closed his eyes and seemed to drift off. Letitia sat alert, stroking his hand.

"He may rest now, just knowing you are here at last," Étienne said.

"I will stay with him in case he wakens again. What did he mean?"

"Just anxious about the business, I suppose. You ought to rest."

"No," said Letitia. "It is you who needs to rest. You have traveled twice as long and hard as I. Just let me sit with him. If he is no worse by dawn, I will perhaps lie down."

Turnbridge appeared in the doorway, his head nearly scraping the lintel.

"He spoke?"

"Yes," Étienne replied. "But he seems to be sleeping now."

Turnbridge nodded. "Can I bring you anything to make you more comfortable?"

"No, thank you. I am fine, sir," said Letitia.

"All right. We've fixed a room for you. Down the hall, last on the right. When you wish to rest, my wife or I will relieve you, and you can get some sleep. If you think he is worse, I'll send for the doctor again."

"Thank you, sir," she said.

Turnbridge nodded and left the room.

Étienne hated to leave her, but he knew the wisdom of taking some rest. He'd slept little the night before and traveled all day. He took an extra candlestick from the dresser and paused by Letitia's side.

"*Bon nuit*, mon amie," he whispered.

"Good night. And thank you for everything."

She looked up into his eyes, and he saw tears threatening. One spilled over and trickled down her cheek, and he could not stay his hand from reaching out to her. He touched her face gently with his palm, brushing the tear away with his thumb.

"Pray, my love." Instantly he knew he had again said too much, and he drew back his hand. "Forgive me. This is not the time."

She grasped his hand and brought it back to rest against her cheek. "We disagree. Can you forgive me for that?"

They looked into each other's sorrowful eyes for a moment, and Étienne swallowed hard. "Always," he said. "And I stand corrected."

❧

Letitia sat watching her father's face. His breathing seemed too rapid and shallow, but she couldn't detect any signs of pain. She sat for hours, and her eyelids drooped. There was no clock in the room. How far away was dawn?

She jerked awake, thinking she must soon call someone to spell her or she would fall off the chair and end up asleep on the hooked rug.

"Letitia."

"Yes, Father." She went eagerly to her knees beside the bed to get closer to him.

"Mark will help you."

"Mark? No, Father, you don't understand. I'm here with you at Turnbridge now. When you are better, we'll go home."

"Mark Warren knows. He will help you. If you don't wish to marry—"

"Father, don't concern yourself about such things now. Be at peace. You need to rest and get your strength."

"No, I sent Steve for a reason." He tossed fitfully beneath the red and white flying geese quilt.

"You sent him to get me. I am here now."

"Yes, daughter."

Letitia stroked his hand.

"Talk to Mark," he said a moment later, without opening his eyes.

"All right, Father. I will."

A growing unease filled her. Her father was worried about something specific. She stayed on her knees on the rug, holding his hand and leaning her head against the side of the bed, where the quilt hung down.

She jerked awake some time later and realized Étienne was kneeling beside her.

"Letitia, dear," he said softly, "Come, ma chérie, you must rest. I will take you to your room."

She stared at him blankly then shifted to look at her father. His breathing was softer, but still rapid, and his face was ashen.

"But Father—"

"Yes, darling," Étienne said. "He is the same."

She turned toward him, unable to stop her tears, and he put his arms around her.

"What time is it?" she asked in a small voice.

"After two o'clock. Dearest Letitia, you need to sleep. I will watch him." He held her head against his shoulder and stroked her silky hair.

Letitia let out a tremulous sigh. Never had she known that a man's strong arms could bring so much comfort. "C–could we pray?"

"Of course." Étienne bowed his head and began, "Our dear Father in heaven." He paused, took a breath, and then hesitated again.

Letitia opened her eyes a crack and peeked up at him.

"I am sorry," he whispered. "I am not accustomed to praying in English."

"Pray in French, then. God will understand you."

His smile all but melted her heart, and he stooped to brush his lips across her forehead. "Thank you, my love, but He will understand my poor English as well." He took a deep breath and closed his eyes once more. "We beg Your healing for this man and Your strength and comfort for his daughter."

She relaxed against him. His cotton shirt smelled fresh and clean, and a trace of the odor of soap lingered where he had obviously shaved earlier.

After his brief prayer, she smiled up at him. "Please don't make me leave, dearest."

Étienne frowned and glanced toward her father's form once more. "If it were my father, I would not want to leave either," he conceded.

When Mrs. Turnbridge came to the door two hours later with a tray of tea, bacon, and biscuits, she smiled at Étienne. He knew it was because he, the lumberman's clerk, was sitting on the rose trellis rug covering the hardwood floor, holding his employer's beautiful daughter, sound asleep, in his arms.

seventeen

The physician returned to Turnbridge Farm just before noon, and Mrs. Turnbridge brought him up to the patient's room, where Étienne was keeping watch. Mrs. Turnbridge had put Letitia to bed hours before, and Étienne had stayed with her father, promising to call her if there was any change.

"He seems feeble, Dr. Bowles," Étienne said, as the man bent over the bed, counting Hunter's heartbeats.

"Yes, he's weaker than he was yesterday."

"Do you think he has a chance of recovery, sir?"

The doctor shook his head. "His heart has betrayed him, young man. You went for his daughter?"

"Yes. She spent the night at his side and is resting now. Do you want to see her?"

"I think she must be prepared," said Bowles.

"Yes, sir."

"I will fetch her," said Mrs. Turnbridge from the doorway. She turned and went down the hallway.

Ten minutes later, Letitia appeared, freshly attired, but with a cast of fatigue still on her face.

"Miss Hunter?" asked the doctor, rising from his chair.

"Yes, sir." She trembled as she stepped forward, and Étienne went to her side.

"You must not have too much hope, my dear," the doctor said. "Your father is very weak, and I cannot say he will rise from this bed again."

Letitia stood still for a moment, then reached out toward Étienne.

He grasped her hand. "Sit down, Letitia," he murmured and drew her to the chair.

159

When she was seated, she looked up at the doctor. "Do you think, sir, with extended rest. . . ?"

Bowles sighed. "Anything is possible, if you believe in God Almighty."

"Oh, I do, sir."

He shrugged. "I do not wish to give you false hope. You cannot move him. That is certain. If he hangs on, he might strengthen; but it would be a matter of weeks, perhaps a month or more."

Letitia turned toward the doorway where Mrs. Turnbridge, in her apron, still hovered.

"Could you keep us, ma'am? I will pay you well for your hospitality."

"Of course," she said. "You may stay as long as there is need. My daughter and I will help care for him. You mustn't trouble yourself about that."

"You understand it's unlikely?" the doctor persisted. "I do not think he will live much longer, though it pains me to be so blunt with you."

"I understand." Letitia turned once more to gaze on her father's ashen face.

"I can do nothing for him. He could slip away anytime."

"Or he might get better?" Letitia asked hopefully.

"Do not hope too much."

"But if I don't—" She sobbed, and Étienne placed his hand on her shoulder.

"I'm sorry I can do no more," said Bowles. He picked up his medical bag. "If he rallies, send me word. If he is worse, well. . .if he is worse, there is nothing I can do, and it will be too late by the time I get here. I'm sorry."

"I understand." Letitia pressed a generous fee on him, and the doctor went on his way.

She stayed in her father's room, and Étienne found another chair in his bedroom and brought it so he could sit with her. The farmer's daughter, Mrs. Clark, brought lunch up for them a short time later, and he urged Letitia to eat, knowing she had taken little in the past twenty-four hours.

Lincoln Hunter lay unmoving, his eyes closed, his skin as pale as the white patches between the triangular red flying geese of the quilt.

"He spoke to me about his lawyer last night," Letitia said, glancing toward Étienne.

"What did he say?"

"Just that I should talk to Mark Warren. Étienne, I felt he was trying to tell me something particular. You were here when he said, 'Don't sell,' and then later he started to say something about my marrying."

"He is concerned for you, in case he is not here to take care of you."

"No, it was more than that. He urged me several times to talk to Mr. Warren."

"Then you should do it."

"Yes, when we go home."

An hour later, Étienne urged her to nap again while he stayed with her father.

"No, I can't bear to leave him now," she said. "You go rest, and I will wake you when I can't keep my eyes open."

"You said that last night," he replied. "If it does not distress you, I will stay awhile."

"Thank you."

He saw relief in her eyes, and he pulled his chair closer to hers and reached for her hand.

"Perhaps I should write a note to Mr. Weston," she said.

"If you wish. It sounds as though you might be here for some time."

"Yes."

"Let me make a proposal," said Étienne. "If in a day or two it looks like your father will have a long convalescence here, I will bear your news to Mr. Weston and Mr. Linden, and I will stay in Zimmerville as your agent."

She looked at him in alarm. "I should hate to see you go. How would I manage without you?"

"I should hate to leave you, too, but one of us needs to be there to watch the business your father has built so painstakingly."

Mr. Hunter moaned, and Letitia flew from her chair. "Father! I am here. Can you hear me?"

"Water," he whispered hoarsely.

Étienne held a glass to Hunter's lips, raising his head and shoulders with a strong arm.

"Daughter."

"Yes, Father." She squeezed his hand and knelt again on the rug, her face inches from his own.

"Letitia, if you don't want to marry him. . ."

"Who, Father?" she cried.

"If you don't like him, don't sell out to him. And you must rely on yourself to find a husband. God knows I've tried."

Letitia sniffed. "I'm sorry, Father. You've always let me refuse any man I didn't care for."

"I don't want to see you unhappy, my dear. But I thought I would see you married. You need a man who—" He closed his eyes and breathed with effort.

"Just rest now. We'll talk about this later," Letitia said quietly, stroking his forehead.

He opened his eyes again. "No, child, there's not time. Northern is a very valuable company."

"Of course, Father."

"It is yours now."

"No, Father, you can't—"

Étienne's hand came down once more on her shoulder, and she looked up at him.

"Let him speak," he said gently.

She turned to her father and whispered, "All right. Dear Father, what is it you wish to tell me?"

Lincoln drew a deep breath. "He spoke to me in April, when he brought the order."

"Who, Father?"

"John—" he gasped.

"Not John Rawley?" Letitia's distress wrenched Étienne's heart.

"Yes. When we went to lunch that day. He asked if he might court you, and I told him he would have to win your affections, because..." Hunter's breath was more ragged. "I will not marry my girl to a man she cannot love."

"Oh, Father, thank you." She buried her face in Étienne's handkerchief and sobbed.

"You didn't like him?" It was a whisper.

"No, Father. He came while you were away. He insulted me. I could never love him."

"Ah, well." He was quiet a moment, his eyelids fluttering down then opening again. "I told you, you may refuse whoever you will. Don't let anyone push you into a marriage you don't want."

"You'll get better," she insisted. "And I won't marry anyone unless—Father, you've said I may refuse anyone I choose."

"Yes, child."

"But may I accept the man of my choosing?" Her face flushed scarlet, and Étienne tightened his hand on her shoulder.

Hunter's breathing was more labored, and confusion crossed his face.

"What?" he gasped. "You have picked a suitor without my help?"

"Y–yes."

Étienne felt her tremble. He dropped to his knees beside her. "Sir, it is me. May I speak to you?"

"Steve?" Hunter blinked at him.

"Yes, sir."

"Help Letitia. You have a good head, Steve. Help her with the business. I'm giving you a raise. Now. Today. You'll be her right hand. But if she marries, her husband will take over."

Étienne hesitated. "Yes, sir, but I have something else to say."

Hunter looked into his eyes then, his breath short and wheezing.

"Speak."

"Sir, I love her. If you would consent, I would take care of her for the rest of my life." He stopped as the older man's eyes flared and his face convulsed.

"Father!" Letitia pushed Étienne aside and stroked her father's brow. "Father, it is enough talk for now. Please don't leave us. Just rest. Don't be upset."

His eyes closed, and each breath seemed a Herculean effort.

"Oh no, oh no." Letitia laid her cheek on the quilt and wept. "I should have kept quiet. Étienne, I shouldn't have said anything, but I love you." Her sobs racked her.

Étienne put one arm around her and smoothed her hair with his other hand.

"Ma chérie, I am sorry. I will do anything for you. I'm so sorry."

"He told you to speak," she quavered.

"Yes. He knows now." Étienne's heart ached with guilt and sorrow. "I don't think he was pleased."

She sobbed once, then took a deep breath. "It is in God's hands."

They sat together for several hours, until the sun dropped low in the west, sending brilliant orange rays through the dormer window onto the white wall beyond. Letitia shifted her position several times, from the rug to the chair to the far edge of the bed. She was sitting in the chair with Étienne beside her when Lincoln's eyes opened again.

"Letitia."

"Yes, Father." She jumped eagerly closer.

"You choose your man. Rawley wants the company, but. . .you must have a man. . .who loves you."

"I do, sir!" Étienne said firmly.

Hunter looked up, searching for him.

"Steve—"

"Yes, sir."

"Don't sell out, Steve."

"Never."

"Then marry her. It is. . .right."

Étienne slipped his arm around Letitia as her father turned his troubled eyes on her.

"I should never have turned away from God. But He knows."

"Yes, He knows and forgives," Letitia whispered.

"I love you, daughter." His eyes closed. He breathed again, then sighed, and the room was still.

"Father!"

"He is gone," Étienne said softly.

Letitia touched her father's cheek then turned slowly. "Étienne."

"Yes, my love."

She put her arms out to him, and he pulled her into his embrace.

"I will take care of you," he promised.

"I know."

She looked up at him, her eyes full of hope and trust; and he bent toward her, his lips meeting hers in the kiss he at last had the right to give. She trembled and slid her arms up around his neck. He held her tightly for a long moment.

At last he said, "I will go tell Mr. Turnbridge, ma chérie, and tomorrow we will take him home."

epilogue

Étienne guided the team toward the Zimmerville train station through the lightly falling snow.

"I'm so glad your mother and the boys could come before Christmas." Letitia scooted over closer to him on the seat, took her hand from her fur muff, and slipped it through his arm.

He smiled down at her. "You get your wish, and we can be married Christmas Eve."

"Do you think Richard and Jean-Claude will be all right alone in the office this afternoon?" she asked. "I'd like it if you could stay at the house with us for a while, but if you think they'll need you..."

"Those boys will be fine," Étienne said. "Jacques will no doubt look in at least twice to make sure his son is not misbehaving while the boss is out."

Letitia smiled. Training Jacques and Angelique's oldest boy to replace her as clerk, along with Richard Shelby, had been a joy. Every day as she and Étienne tutored the two young men in the office routine, they knew the day of Letitia's freedom and their wedding was coming closer.

The train arrived in a flurry of noise and smoke. Étienne scanned the windows anxiously, then touched Letitia's arm and pointed. Soon a small, middle-aged woman and two half-grown boys were climbing down from the passenger car.

"Étienne!" the younger boy cried, running toward them. "You should have been on the train! We went so fast!"

Étienne laughed and stepped forward to assist his mother. Letitia waited for him to greet her privately, but when he turned and beckoned to her, she joined him, glad to meet his mother at last.

"My dear," Madame LeClair murmured with tears in her eyes.

Letitia bent toward her and kissed her cheek. "I'm so happy that you are here, madame."

Étienne's mother turned to him. "*Elle* est belle!"

He chuckled. "Oui, très belle, *Maman*." He quickly introduced his two youngest brothers, Paul and Denis.

"Will André be able to come?" his mother asked him.

"Yes," Étienne told her, "I've written to his foreman at Nine Mile Camp and told him to give André next week off."

She nodded, content. "I wish your sisters could come, but it is just too far."

Letitia smiled. "We wish they could be here, too, but we're overjoyed that you and all the boys will be with us for the ceremony."

Madame LeClair looked anxiously at Étienne. "And after? I did as you said and sold the farm to Elaine and her husband."

"Do not fear, Maman," he told her. "Letitia and I have looked about the town for a small house for you and the boys, and we have made a decision."

"Oh?"

He glanced at Letitia, arching his eyebrows.

Letitia stepped forward and took his mother's hands. "Étienne and I have decided to keep my parents' house. We thought at first we would sell it, as it is very large. Perhaps too large. But then we thought, why sell this big place and buy two smaller houses, one for you and one for us? Why not have you and the boys stay with us?"

"Oh, we do not wish to impose," Madame LeClair said. "You will be newlyweds, after all."

Étienne laughed. "Maman, wait until you see the house. It is so large we will not even know you are there unless you want us to. And besides, I am taking Letitia away for two weeks after the wedding. We need someone to be there in the house and to welcome us when we return."

Madame LeClair looked from him to Letitia, her forehead wrinkled and her brown eyes anxious. "Well, if you are sure."

"We're sure," Étienne said. "But if you try it for a while and you don't like it, we will make other arrangements in the spring."

"Well, I suppose I can help Letitia with the cooking," his mother said.

"We have a cook, Maman, but don't let that scare you. I'm sure Mrs. Watkins will let you into the kitchen if you want to bake an apple tart."

The boys came down the platform hauling several satchels.

A half hour later, they all stood in the parlor of the Hunter mansion. Étienne watched as his mother stared about her. Even Paul and Denis were silenced by the grandeur of the house.

"It is too much," Madame LeClair said.

"But this is Letitia's home, and she loves it very much," Étienne said.

His mother shook her head, staring at the paintings and velvet draperies. "It is so—" She swallowed hard and looked at Letitia. "I am sorry, my dear. It is wonderful. It is just—we are not used to such—"

Letitia touched her sleeve. "I understand. I hope that you will grow to love this home as I do. But if not, we will find you a little house of your own, I promise."

"Come, boys, I will show you your rooms," Étienne said.

"We get our own rooms?" Denis asked. He and Paul stared at each other.

"Yes, but they have a door between," said Étienne.

"And I will take you up to your room, dear mother," said Letitia. "Agnes will bring your bags and help you unpack."

"Wait," said Madame LeClair. "I have here a box for you, Letitia."

She held out a parcel tied with string.

"Why, thank you." Letitia took it, and Étienne brought out

his pocketknife to cut the string.

She laid the box on a cherry side table and opened it, lifting out a filmy shower of ethereal lace.

"Oh, it's lovely!"

Madame LeClair smiled at her oldest son. "I went to Madame Rousseau, as you instructed me."

"The same lady who made the table runner you sent for my birthday?" Letitia asked him.

"Yes. I asked Maman to see if she would make you a wedding veil."

"It's the most beautiful creation in the world," Letitia said.

&a.

On Christmas Eve, Étienne paced a small anteroom in the little church. His brother, André, who had arrived on the Bangor train the night before, slouched in a chair, watching him with glittering eyes. Jacques Laplante and René Ouellette straightened each other's neckties.

"What time is it?" Étienne asked.

"Relax, mon ami," said René. "They will tell us when it is time."

At that moment the pastor entered. "Come," he said to Étienne. "It is time."

André went to escort their mother to the seat of honor, and Étienne and his friends stood at the front of the church.

The pews were filled with the church members, the employees of Northern Lumber, many of the company's customers, and the Hunter family's old acquaintances. Étienne felt sweat beading on his brow, although the sanctuary was cool.

The organist began to play, and all eyes turned to the back of the church. Sophie and Angelique entered, walking slowly the length of the aisle. Jacques and René beamed at their wives, who wore the simple but lovely gowns Letitia had ordered sewn for them. Finally came Letitia, on the arm of attorney Mark Warren.

Étienne caught his breath. Through the sheer lace veil he

could see her bright eyes on him and her radiant smile. At last she was by his side, and Mr. Warren gave her over into his care. With her hand cradled in his, he faced the pastor, ready to conquer the world.

He repeated the simple vows looking into her eyes, knowing that finally he had the right to say them and to claim her. "I, Étienne, take thee, Letitia, to be my lawfully wedded wife."

Her voice breathless, she took her vows, and he slipped the plain gold ring onto her finger. Angelique stepped forward and laid back the intricate lace veil. Étienne stooped to kiss his bride. If not for her joyful smile, he would have thought this moment an impossible dream.

She clung to him for a moment and whispered, "I love you."

He smiled down at her. "*Je t'aime*, ma chérie."

A Letter To Our Readers

Dear Reader:

In order that we might better contribute to your reading enjoyment, we would appreciate your taking a few minutes to respond to the following questions. We welcome your comments and read each form and letter we receive. When completed, please return to the following:

Fiction Editor
Heartsong Presents
PO Box 719
Uhrichsville, Ohio 44683

1. Did you enjoy reading *The Lumberjack's Lady* by Susan Page Davis?
   ❏ Very much! I would like to see more books by this author!
   ❏ Moderately. I would have enjoyed it more if

   _____

   _____

   _____

2. Are you a member of **Heartsong Presents**? ❏ Yes ❏ No
   If no, where did you purchase this book? _____

   _____

3. How would you rate, on a scale from 1 (poor) to 5 (superior), the cover design? _____

4. On a scale from 1 (poor) to 10 (superior), please rate the following elements.

   ____ Heroine   ____ Plot
   ____ Hero   ____ Inspirational theme
   ____ Setting   ____ Secondary characters

5. These characters were special because? _____

_____

_____

6. How has this book inspired your life? _____

_____

_____

7. What settings would you like to see covered in future
   Heartsong Presents books? _____

_____

_____

8. What are some inspirational themes you would like to see
   treated in future books? _____

_____

_____

9. Would you be interested in reading other **Heartsong
   Presents** titles? ❏ Yes ❏ No

10. Please check your age range:
    ❏ Under 18   ❏ 18-24
    ❏ 25-34   ❏ 35-45
    ❏ 46-55   ❏ Over 55

Name _____

Occupation _____

Address _____

City, State, Zip _____

Hearts♥ng